"I have reason to think that Jason is my son."

Ben's words, though barely uttered, ricocheted off the walls of Dory's mind like gunshots fired at close range.

"Y-you don't know what you're saying. What on earth makes you think such a thing?"

The initial fear his insane declaration inspired rapidly gave way to anger as Dory's maternal instincts came rushing to the surface, and her expression changed from vulnerable to belligerent in a matter of seconds.

This was not the teary-eyed response Ben had expected. With her face flushed with color and those green eyes blazing at him, Dory looked more beautiful than he'd ever seen her. To his dismal surprise, he found himself wanting her again, this time more fiercely that he had a right to.

Dear Reader,

Welcome to another month of powerhouse reading here at Silhouette Intimate Moments. Start yourself off with Lindsay Longford's *Renegade's Redemption*. Who doesn't love to read about a rough, tough loner who's saved by the power of a woman's love?

Move on to Susan Mallery's *Surrender in Silk*. This sensuous read takes a heroine whose steely exterior hides the vulnerable woman beneath and matches her with the only man who's ever reached that feminine core—the one man she's sure she shouldn't love. Alexandra Sellers plays with one of the most powerful of the traditional romantic fantasies in *Bride of the Sheikh*. Watch as heroine Alinor Brooke is kidnapped from her own wedding—by none other than the desert lord who's still her legal husband! In *Framed*, Karen Leabo makes her heroine the prime suspect in an apparent murder, but her hero quickly learns to look beneath the surface of this complicated case— and this fascinating woman. Nancy Morse returns with *A Child of His Own*, a powerfully emotional tale of what it really means to be a parent. And finally, welcome new author Debra Cowan. In *Dare To Remember* she spins a romantic web around the ever-popular concept of amnesia.

Read and enjoy them all—and then come back next month for more of the most exciting romantic reading around, here at Silhouette Intimate Moments.

Yours,

Leslie Wainger

Leslie Wainger
Senior Editor and Editorial Coordinator

Please address questions and book requests to:
Silhouette Reader Service
U.S.: 3010 Walden Ave., P.O. Box 1325, Buffalo, NY 14269
Canadian: P.O. Box 609, Fort Erie, Ont. L2A 5X3

A CHILD OF HIS OWN

NANCY MORSE

Silhouette®
INTIMATE™ MOMENTS®

Published by Silhouette Books

America's Publisher of Contemporary Romance

SILHOUETTE BOOKS

ISBN 0-373-07773-4

A CHILD OF HIS OWN

Copyright © 1997 by Nancy Morse

Books by Nancy Morse

Silhouette Intimate Moments

Sacred Places #181
Run Wild, Run Free #210
The Mom Who Came To Stay #683
A Child of His Own #773

NANCY MORSE

Born and raised in New York City, Nancy has lived for the last three years in Florida with her husband of twenty-eight years, Talley, and their Alaskan Malamute, Max. An early love of reading and happy endings led to the publication of her first historical romance in 1980. She has an avid interest in Native American history and culture, and takes great pride in her collection of nineteenth-century artifacts. In addition to writing, Nancy enjoys gardening, watching good films, reading and regular aerobic workouts to sweat out the daily frustrations of life.

clothing store in Woodstock. He'd gotten the piece of

Chapter 1

Ben heard a cry in the woods.

He sat bolt upright in his narrow sleeping bag, listening, staring into the misty forest. A shudder ran through his body as he drew the sides of the sleeping bag closer about him. He waited, straining to hear, but the cry didn't come again. His pulse pounded at his temples. It must have been his own voice he had heard crack the dawn stillness.

Rubbing the sleep from his eyes, Ben shimmied out of the warmth of his cocoon and rose. The chill April air nipped at his nakedness as he groped for his jeans. With an absentminded flick of the finger he swept back a lock of dark hair that spilled across his brow. His forehead was damp to the touch, confirming what he already suspected; he'd had that awful dream again.

Dressed in jeans and a turtleneck, he shrugged into the brown leather flight jacket he'd found in a vintage clothing store in Woodstock. He'd gotten the piece of

World War II nostalgia for a song, and a good thing it was, since he didn't have much more than that in his pocket at the time.

The worn cowhide brought to mind images of flying aces and the model P-51 Mustang bombers with their beautiful bullet-nosed propellers that he used to make out of balsa as a boy. It was funny, really, but these days nothing much thrilled him, except perhaps the memory of those model P-51s.

After a breakfast of ham and eggs at a roadside inn, curiosity at a help-wanted sign he'd seen posted at the diner led Ben down a narrow, winding road, to a spot off the beaten path.

A smile sprouted on his face as he rounded the bend and got his first glimpse of the place, but it quickly faded as he drew closer and saw the run-down, ramshackled look of peeling paint.

It was an amusement park, or what was left of it. The grounds were disturbingly silent in the morning sunshine, the games of chance quietly collecting dust, shrouds of tarpaulin draped over the carousel. An unexplained shiver coursed over Ben's flesh at the absence of life in an atmosphere that should have been filled with fun and laughter.

He followed a worn path around back to a two-story clapboard house. The steps creaked when he climbed them to the porch. The screen door rattled when he knocked on its frame.

Through the screen he saw a man approach, the agility of his step belying the aged face that greeted him through the mesh.

"Yes? Can I help you?"

Ben moved a little to the side in case his face was hidden in shadow. "How do you do, sir?" he said politely. "My name is Ben Stone." The breath caught in his throat as he waited to see what reaction that brought, but when the old man just looked at him as if the name meant nothing at all, Ben sighed inwardly with relief, and added, "I was wondering if you could use some help around here."

The old man's eyes sparkled beneath a shelf of white brows. "You don't look as if you're from around here," he observed.

"No, sir, I'm not."

"Just passing through, are you?"

"You could say that."

The funny thing was, he'd come to like it that way, finding a strange kind of comfort in his solitary drifter's existence. If he didn't like a place, he simply moved on. No questions, no explanations, no regrets. He'd found that he could survive by doing odd jobs in exchange for room and board. He kept away from the urban areas where there was always the chance that somebody might recognize him from the newspaper reports of the trial. He preferred the anonymity of the backroads and the folks he met along the way who were friendlier, less likely to judge, and, like this old guy, not so apt to remember. At times he himself could almost forget the circumstances that had led him to his drifter's existence. Until night fell, that is, and that cursed dream came back to remind him.

Ben backed away from the door. "If you don't have any work for me, I'll be on my way."

"Hold on there, young fella." The screen door opened and a lean and lanky figure stepped onto the porch. "Who said we don't have any work for you? When can you start?"

"Start what?"

A feminine voice from behind snapped Ben's head around.

She had grease on her cheek and a wrench in her hand. The forthright manner in which she strode toward them made Ben take a step back. For an instant she looked as if she was about to hit him with the wrench, but then, to a man who'd spent three years confined to a cell, every little movement seemed larger than life.

Ben's uneasiness lasted only a moment. At first he didn't know what produced the easing in his muscles. Then he realized it was her eyes. They were a deep, dark green, like the sea, with lashes that were long and uncommonly straight, swooping down and hiding, almost, the look of sadness which his own keen eyes detected. In spite of the menacing wrench, something in those eyes told Ben this woman wouldn't hurt a fly. She was too scared. And too lovely to suit him.

It wasn't the kind of beauty that reached out and grabbed a man by the throat. It was the quiet kind which, once it attracted the eye, did not relinquish it easily, as Ben was already finding out. Sunlight and shadow were the only makeup on her face. Her chestnut hair was pulled back in an uncomplicated ponytail, accentuating smooth cheekbones and the slant of her eyes. A few curly rebels escaped the tie to slash across her face in the April breeze, one burnished strand tangling in her lashes.

She was wearing loose-fitting jeans that were frayed at the knees and a white V-neck T-shirt that revealed a triangle of pale flesh untouched by the sun. Something inside of Ben tightened at the sight of her smooth skin, and he caught himself wondering if the rest of her was as soft and white as that little bit of flesh.

Suddenly, he was acutely and unwelcomingly aware of how long it had been since he'd been with a woman.

"Start what?" she asked again, her sea-green eyes fixed anxiously on the old man.

"Work. Just this morning you were complaining that there's so much to do around here in so short a time, weren't you?"

In a soft voice, she said hesitatingly, "Well, yes, but—"

"And this young man is in need of employment."

Those green eyes shifted uncomfortably to Ben and assessed him for several moments.

His hair was dark, his eyes darker. His face was fine-boned and handsome, with a steeliness about it that suggested something quick and dangerous. He was lean and angular, with broad, powerfully built shoulders beneath the brown leather jacket and wiry muscles encased in formfitting denim.

He was the kind of man who brought about an immediate response in a woman, yet experience had taught Dory to be wary of men. Her fingers tightened instinctively around the wrench.

"I'm sorry, Mr....?"

"Stone. Ben Stone," the old man offered. "Sorry for my manners." He thrust his hand out to Ben. "I'm Martin Jones, and this is my granddaughter, Dory McBride."

"Grandfather," she said, "I don't think Mr. Stone would be interested in the kind of work we need done."

"Why not let him decide that for himself?"

Turning to Ben, she said, "There must be a misunderstanding. We don't need help."

Ben glanced around pointedly. "You could've fooled me."

A flicker of pain darted through her eyes. "It's true that the Dutch Mill has seen better times."

"I saw the sign you posted in town," he said, "so I figured I'd give it a try."

"The sign, yes. Well, you see, I had someone a little more...that is, a little less... Actually, I thought that maybe one of the local schoolkids... The truth is, Mr. Stone, that I couldn't pay you very much."

Ben's dark eyes never left her face, assessing the smudge of grease on her smooth cheek, and the tender ache he saw in her green eyes. *Move on,* he told himself. *Pick up your bag and keep right on going.* Instead, he heard himself say, "Maybe we can work something out."

Dory bit the corner of her bottom lip, and ventured, "What do you have in mind?"

"Judging from this—" he reached up and wiped the grease from her cheek with the tip of his thumb "—I'd say something needs fixing."

Dory's skin jumped at the unexpected heat of his touch. "I'm trying to get the Dutch Mill ready to open on Memorial Day."

"From the looks of things, you have your work cut out for you. Tell you what, I'll stick around and help you get ready for opening day in exchange for room and board."

Dory drew back. She didn't want to hire him. She didn't need or want a man around, especially a man like him, a drifter, a loner—someone she knew very little about. Still, it was a tempting offer.

The income from the Dutch Mill had kept the place going from year to year, but a fire three years ago had put them temporarily out of business. The insurance money and their savings were more than enough to put the Dutch Mill back together again, but Dory knew she couldn't do it alone, not if she wanted to open on Memorial Day.

She looked skeptically into Ben's dark eyes. "You would work for nothing? Why would you do that for people you don't even know?"

It was easy to see that she didn't trust him, and he wondered what she would think if she knew he'd spent three years in prison. He warned himself to be careful. He couldn't risk revealing too much. Yet the thought of spending a few nights in a warm bed instead of on the hard earth was appealing.

"I'm not doing it for you. I'm doing it for myself. I can use a place to stay, and this is as good a place as any."

Dory looked at Martin, her eyes searching his seamed face for an answer to her dilemma.

Martin smiled tenderly and caressed her cheek with the back of a veined hand. "You really mustn't worry so much," he said. "Nothing is so bad, Dory, that it can't be made better."

Ben watched the exchange between them and saw the unconvinced half smile she gave her grandfather, and again he found himself wondering at the sadness he sensed about her. Behind those pretty green eyes and quiet beauty lurked a sorrow, a memory perhaps, of some lingering hurt.

It was in her voice also, a tinge of melancholy beneath the softly spoken words, when she turned back to him and said, "I wouldn't think of not paying you. How's fifty dollars a week?"

"Sounds good to me," he replied.

To Martin she said, "I'll give Mrs. Norton a call to find out what time you have to pick up Jason. Meanwhile, would you show Mr. Stone to the spare room?" With a skeptical look she disappeared inside the house.

As Ben trailed Martin upstairs, a glance around revealed simple, staightforward furnishings. A roll-arm sofa in a pretty floral print sat before a woodburning stove, a crocheted afghan spread over its back. It was flanked by an easy chair whose arms were worn with use and whose seat dipped a little from the weight of its favorite occupant. A carpet of cinnabar and black was spread over the hardwood floor.

On the walls were hung family photographs. There was a picture of Martin and a pretty woman, his wife probably, Ben surmised, from the loving look in Martin's eyes. There was a man and a woman standing proudly before a carousel, with a little girl between them. But it was the picture of a small boy that brought an unconscious smile to Ben's lips and had him looking back over his shoulder as he followed Martin up the stairs.

The room to which he was shown was comfortable and inviting with its chenille bedspread and the old, oak furnishings glistening from furniture polish.

He hung his jacket on a hanger in the closet. What little else he owned fit neatly into one dresser drawer. When he finished unpacking, he went to the window to look out.

In the distance the Catskill Mountains heralded the arrival of spring with rolling carpets of green. An early morning fog rose from a cobweb of streams and settled in hollows of the rich, rolling farmland below. The foothills were dotted with flowering dogwoods.

He stood there for a long time, gazing at the sun-dappled trees, and marveling at how swiftly life changed with a single turn in the road. He wondered a little guiltily what Martin Jones and his pretty grand-daughter would think if they knew his background. Safe to say, he'd be out of a job before he even got to the end of the story. The old man seemed friendly enough, but the granddaughter wasn't. He'd gotten the distinct impression that she felt she had gone against her better judgment in hiring him. He knew from experience that most people had an aversion to ex-cons, no matter what the circumstances, so the less they knew about his past, the better.

He'd be the first to admit that it was bizarre. One day he'd been a successful architect, partner in one of Manhattan's leading firms, the next day, imprisoned for the brutal beating of his wife, only to be pardoned three years later when her jealous lover murdered her, then confessed also to the earlier crime that had sent the wrong man to jail.

Ben smothered a bitter laugh in his throat. They owed him a lot more than a pardon; they owed him his life back. But that, he knew with cold certainty, would never happen. His life, as he knew it, ended that fateful Christmas Eve when Allison knocked on his door.

They'd been separated for months and divorce had been inevitable, when she'd shown up at his apartment claiming she missed him. Somehow, they found themselves together intimately one last time. Old time's sake, she called it. For Ben it had been one lonely hour of need that would change his life forever.

Five months later, fed up with her constant demands for money, he'd gone to see her, determined to have

it out with her once and for all, and had been shocked
to find her pregnant. He'd wondered if the child were
his, then some quick calculations brought him back to
Christmas Eve. His fingers whitened around the win-
dowsill as he recalled the gut-shaking anger he'd felt
when she told him that, in order to make some money,
she had made arrangements to put the baby up for a
private adoption. He thought his threat to cut her off
without a penny would deter her from going through
with her plan, but he realized how wrong he was several weeks later, when she was found badly beaten.
Then she did the unthinkable—she named him as her
attacker in order to get him out of the picture and
proceed with her plan.

He'd lost count of the untold hours he'd spent agonizing over the mistake he had made in marrying her.
He could scarcely recall the reason. Love? Looking
back, he realized that he had just assumed that what
he felt for Allison was love. She was beautiful and
ambitious, a complement to his skyrocketing career,
or so he had thought. At first they'd been happy. The
more money he earned in his climb to the top of his
profession, the more she spent. It wasn't the spending
sprees he minded, though. It was the infidelities.

The first time it happened he masked his pain and
tried to understand. After all, he worked so much, and
she was alone so often, and human, so very human.
But it happened again and again, pushing his understanding to the brink of anger, and finally, to full-
blown fury. He never guessed, when he had threatened
to cut her off without a penny, to what lengths she
would go when backed into a corner.

A blur of events had ensued. There'd been sirens
and people pointing fingers, a prosecutor and a jury,

and three years of living hell that no pardon could ever erase.

The first thing he did when he was released from prison was go to the office of the attorney who had arranged the adoption, only to have his hopes of claiming his child painfully dashed. Not having come forward within six months of the adoption, to his despair he learned that he had terminated his parental rights. He could still recall the feeling of utter desolation that had accompanied the news. Then he saw a glimmer of hope, like a ray of pale light at the end of a pitch-black tunnel, when an unwitting clerk let it slip that the child was a boy, and that he was living somewhere in the upstate New York area.

Since that day, his search for his son had taken him from the Hudson River Valley to the Adirondack Mountains, from the Finger Lakes clear to the Canadian border, and now here, to this peaceful green valley in the Catskills.

Ben drew a breath of crisp spring air into his lungs. All those years he'd spent amid the teeming humanity of New York City, he never realized that this kind of beauty existed so close to home. Whoever would have guessed that the white-as-milk, clapboard houses and steepled churches of the surrounding towns and hamlets were only a few hours away from his former existence? There was a calm up here unlike anything he'd ever known, an elixir for his bruised senses, and a feeling of unbounding freedom that only a man who has spent years in prison could truly understand.

The sound of the screen door downstairs brought Ben's thoughts back from the painful past to the uncertain present. A figure leaving the house caught his attention.

She moved with long-legged grace down the narrow dirt path, unconscious of the eyes that watched from the second-story window, her ponytail brushing her shoulders in ribbons of golden light that slanted through the branches of the trees.

He had to admire her courage. Getting the Dutch Mill up and running by Memorial Day was no small task. But it was more than her courage that intrigued him. Her composure was compelling. As they had stood on the wide weathered planks of the porch, her calm had remained unbroken. Had she been enraged? Surprised? It had been impossible for him to tell as he had looked into those sad and unsettling eyes. For a reason unknown to him, he'd been torn by an impulse to put his arms around her and comfort her.

Now, as he watched her slender figure duck and disappear beneath the tarpaulin that covered the carousel, he was seized by a much more primal urge. He shook off the unnerving sensation and turned from the window. He'd learned in prison to suppress those kinds of emotions, and habits learned behind bars were hard habits to break.

Chapter 2

The Catskills weren't really mountains at all, but a landmass uplifted and scoured by glaciers into gentle peaks carpeted in spruce, hemlock, birch, maple and oak. They were green, soothing peaks, created not for scaling, but for gazing upon from the front porch.

This was the land of Rip van Winkle, where the legend of a headless horseman threw fear into travelers of dark and lonely roads, where places like Woodstock stood out in the hearts and minds of a generation, and where, surrounded by hills on the western edge of the Catskills, the Dutch Mill was.

Thousands of tiny dust particles danced in the early afternoon sunshine that slanted through a hole in the roof of the carousel. It fell in soft golden light across the face of the woman who worked amid the prancing horses.

The warmth that teased the air only yesterday had vanished like a fickle friend. In its place was a nip that sent a battalion of goose bumps marching across Dory's flesh and turned the tip of her nose cold. Engrossed in her work, however, she was unaware of the chill as she dipped the paintbrush into the can of vermilion.

With a hand as steady as a surgeon's, she touched up the paint on the martingale adorning one of the spirited stallions. Carved from solid mahogany and carefully finished with special, aged patinas, it had sustained only minor damage in the fire that had destroyed two of its companions and a portion of the carousel roof. Dory had polished its eyes of glass, fastened a new tail of real horse hair, and restored it to its classic ornate design.

As she applied the finishing touch to the scarlet strap that passed between the stallion's forelegs, she tried not to think about the fire that nearly had destroyed the carousel. Yet even though her thoughts were focused on the precision of her work, in the deep dark recesses of her consciousness it lingered, the memory that never went away and that made every moment a painful one, even ones such as this when she was relaxed and engrossed in her work.

Her gaze lifted involuntarily and moved down the row of horses. Most on this side of the carousel had sustained some damage. Some were in worse shape than others. Two of them had been reduced to ashes by the angry flames. That they hadn't all been lost was thanks to the miracle of the sudden, furious downpour that had extinguished the flames and saved the carousel from destruction.

It took a good deal of courage for Dory to bring herself to begin the restoration process. The petting zoo and games of chance simply weren't enough to draw the crowds. It was the carousel that brought people from miles around. Many of the folks who brought their children had ridden these horses in their youth.

Dory's own childhood memories were centered around the gaily painted ponies, the lilting calliope music and the brass ring. As a little girl growing up, she had always known she would one day run the Dutch Mill just as her parents had done. The carousel was one of the oldest in the country, the horses hand-carved in the early 1900s in what was now a lost art. An art major in college, she had acquired the skills to restore the damaged horses to their original splendid condition, with their nostrils flaring, eyes gleaming with a touch of wildness, thick manes flying in an imagined wind. The colors on their flanks were rich and deep. Their harnesses were studded with jewels. Their hooves flashed with gold leaf.

She had scoured the antique shops in the neighboring counties in search of horses to replace the two that had been destroyed in the fire. So far she'd found just one. The new arrival wasn't the same as her beloved old friend, but under her deft hands it had been made to look just as splendid.

It had taken hours upon hours of work, weeks upon weeks of sore muscles and aching joints, of eyes straining to see by lanternlight in the dead of night when Martin and Jason were asleep. The harsh Northeastern winter prevented her from getting much work done on the carousel, but with the shift of the season, trees dusted with green and the brooks running fast with melted snow, she picked up where she'd left off in the fall. When work on the horses was finished, there was the hole in the roof to repair.

There were times when she wanted to throw down

the paintbrush and just walk away, but she didn't. No matter how painful or exhausting it was for her, the carousel was their bread and butter and had to be restored. Besides, the ever-haunting memory of the night of the fire would be with her no matter what she did. She might as well keep on with her work.

These days, heavy shrouds of tarpaulin concealed the damaged portion of the carousel and gave Dory the privacy she needed to do the restoration work, and the solitude to be alone with her memories.

She knew she wasn't to blame for Eddie's death. It would have been suicide to rush headlong into the flames to try to save him. If she felt any blame, it was for not having been able to make their marriage work. If she felt any guilt, it came from the relief of having him gone.

Eddie had always been a restless man. Soon after they were married, he lost interest in running the Dutch Mill. He tried his hand at a series of jobs, none of which he held for very long. At one time he had wanted a child, and when they adopted Jason, he seemed happy and about to settle down at last.

For a girl born and raised in these low, rolling New York mountains dotted with dairy farms, trout streams, small towns and steepled churches, Dory was content to wake up happy each morning, and for a while she did, until that old restless feeling came back to Eddie with a vengeance.

Things started to go bad after that. Eddie soon lost all interest in family life. At first Dory blamed the increasing trouble between them on his heavy drinking. Then she blamed it on herself. After a while there was no one left to blame.

She could blame it on bad timing, rotten luck, or

anything else for that matter, but in her heart, Dory knew it really came down to a case of poor judgment on her part when she married Eddie McBride.

Dory was unaware that the paintbrush had begun to tremble in her hand, until a drop of scarlet paint fell from the tip of the brush and trickled like warm blood down the stallion's chest. With a gasp she let the brush fall from her shaking fingers. In her haste to pick it up, she knocked over the can of paint, sending a stream of bright red spreading across the floor of the carousel. Muttering under her breath, she knelt down to wipe up the spill.

When she had cleaned up the last of the paint, Dory lifted the tarpaulin and stepped down from the carousel into the noonday sunshine. Her half-smothered gasp was lost in the sudden, inexplicable quickening of her pulse at the sight of Ben coming toward her.

"I finished greasing the rides," he said, "and was wondering what Martin wants me to do next."

She swept an errant strand of chestnut hair from her face. "Why would you need Martin to tell you that?"

Her movements were graceful and composed, and thoroughly entrancing in their unhurried, unrehearsed way. They were not without their effect on Ben, who shrugged and replied, "He owns the place, doesn't he?"

"What gave you that impression?"

"I just assumed—" he began.

"The sign out front says P. Jones, Proprietor," she said. "That's me. Dory is short for Pandora." She lifted her slender shoulders in an expression that seemed to say "go figure," and explained, "My parents had a thing for Greek mythology."

"That explains the *P*," he said. "But I thought Martin said your name is McBride."

She should have known that something like that would not escape his notice. There was something a little too sharp in those dark eyes that told her he was no ordinary drifter. On the contrary, she suspected that there wasn't anything ordinary about Ben Stone at all.

"McBride was my husband's name."

"Was?"

"I'm a widow." Inwardly, she pleaded for no more questions. To her relief, there weren't any, only a long, hard probing from those dark eyes, which was almost as bad.

Dory felt like a fly caught in the web of Ben's stare. She knew it was crazy, but when he looked at her, she had the queerest feeling that he could see right through her, clear past her defenses to the core of her regrets.

The sound of her grandfather's voice, accompanied by a child's laughter, diverted their attention. Dory's face broke into a grin. "Are they back already? I swear, this morning has flown by as if on wings." She was waiting, arms open wide, for the little boy who ran to her.

"Mommy! Guess what we did at playschool today. We made a fort out of a big box, and it had windows and everything, and I helped make it."

Dory smiled sweetly and said, "I'll bet it's a great fort, too. Jason, honey, why don't you say hello to Ben. He'll be working here for a little while."

"Hi."

A small round face beamed up at Ben and a tiny hand thrust out to him. At first, he didn't quite know what to do with it. Then, feeling a little awkward and uncharacteristically shy, he reached down. The little hand disappeared in his own big strong one as he accepted the boy's handshake.

"Are you gonna be here the day we open? My mommy said I can ride one of the horses that go up and down. Maybe you can, too."

Ben looked down into that guileless face and didn't know how to tell him that it was his intention to stay only a week or two. He had his own reasons for wanting to move on, reasons that had to do with a little fellow just like this one, although there was something about this tyke that filled him with a sudden longing.

From out of nowhere an unfamiliar feeling welled up inside of him. It was strange and powerful and fleeting, and left Ben wondering what it was about this little boy that had him feeling so unexpectedly fatherly. Probably it had something to do with the fact that his kid would be about this age. But it was like nothing Ben had ever felt before. My God, he thought, if he felt something like this for this little stranger, what sort of emotions would he have for his own son? The realization that those kinds of feelings existed deep within hit him like a ton of bricks. The enchanting little face that beamed up at him made him acutely aware of how little he really knew about being a father, something he had never really taken into consideration when he had embarked on his search for his son.

"Pop-Pop's gonna show me the pollywogs," the boy squealed with delight. "Wanna come?"

"I've tried to explain to Jason that Martin is *my* Pop-Pop," Dory explained to Ben, "but his young mind doesn't quite grasp the concept of great-grandfathers. As far as he's concerned, Martin is his Pop-Pop and that's all there is to it." Turning back to the boy, she said, "Sorry, sweetie pie, but Ben has work to do. You run along."

She sent him skipping back to Martin. "Go on, you two," she called to them, "but be back in one hour for lunch."

Jason could tell time and was eager to prove it every chance he got. She watched proudly as he tugged on Martin's sleeve for a look at his wristwatch. Screwing up his face, he concentrated on the numbers until they were fixed in his mind. Beaming up at Martin, Jason proceeded with his great-grandfather down the path that led to a stream where the newly hatched polly-wogs awaited.

Dory felt a gentle tugging on her heartstrings. Jason was the one bright spot in her life, the beacon that guided her through the dark waters of the past. She had lost a marriage, but she still had Jason. Feeling secure in the thought that nothing and no one would ever take him away from her, she turned back to Ben.

He tried to mask his emotions as he watched the boy disappear around the bend and felt the deep and desperate loneliness that came from wanting his own child. "That's a cute kid you've got there. How old is he?"

"Jason will be five this September," she said proudly. "Do you have any children?"

Remembering bitterly that he had missed the first five years of his own son's childhood, he swallowed down the lump in his throat and said, "No, no chil-dren." He couldn't tell her about that without telling her also about Allison and the rest of it. If she knew he'd spent three years in prison, he'd be out of a job. Not that it should matter to him. He'd gotten used to a haphazard existence. Yet for some strange reason it did matter. He didn't want to lose this job. Something about this place piqued his curiosity. Something about the boy aroused new and frightening feelings. Something about the woman touched a cord deep inside.

He envied the easy, natural way she had with the boy, and the love that seemed as genuine and as real as the air she breathed. When the time came...*if* the time ever came...he hoped he could be as good a father as she was a mother. But then, she'd had almost five years of experience at it, whereas he was a novice, with nothing to go on except his own fears.

He nodded in the direction Martin and Jason had gone, and remarked, "The boy must miss his father."

"Jason was just a baby when Eddie died. He doesn't even remember him."

"You must show him pictures, though, so that he'll remember."

"Yes, I've shown him pictures."

"It must be rough for a kid growing up without knowing his father. Maybe seeing pictures of someone who looks like him helps him feel somehow more connected." He had noticed the lack of resemblance between Dory and the boy and naturally assumed the boy looked like his father.

"It's hardly likely that Jason will see himself if he looks at pictures of Eddie," she said. "Jason's adopted."

Adopted? A stillness came over Ben as the word sank slowly into his brain. That would explain the lack of resemblance between Jason and Dory, and lend some credence to the sudden, jolting feeling that said maybe...just maybe this was the son he was looking for.

The thought was fleeting before Ben dismissed it as

utterly ridiculous. So what if Jason was adopted? It was a coincidence, that's all. Surely, it had nothing to do with him. Yet still the thought persisted. What if the possibility he dared not voice was, indeed, possible? What incredible irony that would be. But then, his life was filled with strange and incredible ironies.

Like the self-contradictory irony that had him thinking that maybe he would stick around a little longer than he had planned. While the prospect of fatherhood frankly scared him, another part of him reasoned that it couldn't hurt to get to know this boy a little better.

"They'll be all right, won't they?" he heard himself ask. He was surprised by the note of impulsive concern he heard in his own voice.

"They've only gone to the stream," she assured him as she turned and began to walk away.

Ben forced his gaze away from the spot where the old man and the small boy had disappeared into the woods and followed Dory back to the carousel.

Gesturing at the shrouds that partially covered the carousel, he inquired, "What's with the tarpaulins?"

"I'm in the process of restoring some of the horses. You know, wear and tear, the elements," she said offhandedly, not wanting to have to explain about the fire and Eddie.

"I can give you a hand with it." He took a step forward and was about to climb up onto the carousel.

She spoke up quickly to stop him. "No, that's all right. There's paint all over the place, and the paint on one of the horses is still wet. You can mend the fence in the petting zoo. One of the goats got out this morning."

She was scared. He could tell by the way she didn't look at him as she spoke. He'd seen the look of fear on the faces of enough men in prison to recognize it on her lovely face, and to know that there was something she didn't want him to know.

"Sure, Dory," he said, backing away. "I'll go mend the fence." The muscles flexed in his broad back as he walked off.

She hadn't lied to him, yet neither had she been truthful. Her conscience was smarting an hour later as she swirled the brush in a can of paint remover, wiped the bristles clean, and stood back to admire her work. It had taken hours to finish this particular horse, a job that would have taken a lot longer if Ben weren't helping with everything else. Despite her initial misgivings, she had to admit that hiring him had been a smart move. Stronger than any high school kid, his size and strength would come in handy when there were heavy jobs to be done. If only he didn't have the unnerving ability to unhinge her with little more than a look.

It wasn't that she was afraid of him, for it wasn't fear he inspired. She sensed an inherent gentleness about him in spite of the dark, mysterious eyes. She saw it earlier in the respectful way in which he had treated Martin. Rather, Dory's fear sprang from within herself, for it reminded her that although she was a woman with a woman's hungers, she could not risk involvement.

With the dismal failure of her former relationship still fresh in her mind, she shored up her defenses against the handsome drifter, not daring to hope for any happiness beyond what she could create for herself and her son right here at the Dutch Mill.

She found Ben at the little enclosure she called the petting zoo, repairing the hole in the fence through which the goat had made its escape. For several moments she said nothing, using his preoccupation with his work to watch him.

He had discarded his jacket and dressed in jeans and a T-shirt, he seemed oblivious to the cool air. An unexpected little thrill coursed through her at the sight of the corded flesh that spanned his well-defined biceps, the breadth of his shoulders, the expanse of his chest, the dark, heavy curls that flicked about his forehead in the breeze.

The graceful movements of his hands, combined with the total symmetry of his body, stirred in Dory an unwelcome feeling of attraction.

Stuffing her hands in her pockets, she stepped forward to announce her presence. Her voice was husky, a little tentative, and unerringly provocative in its quiet way.

"I'm sorry for the way I acted before. It's just that..." She paused, uncertain of just what to say. Then she remembered something Martin always said, having appropriated it from Mark Twain. When in doubt, tell the truth. "Things are difficult enough with just me in there."

Into his nostrils wafted the intoxicating scent of fresh-cut flowers that seemed to accompany her everywhere. His head came up from his work and he fixed a long, steady look at her.

The sunlight sparkled on her chestnut hair, highlighting select strands with gold, others with red. She was wearing it loose now and the thick mane fell to her shoulders in a deep, rich mass. Ben's fingers twitched involuntarily at his sides, tingling with the anticipation of what it must feel like to bury themselves in all that glorious hair.

"Apology accepted," he said.

"I've been working like the devil trying to get the carousel ready for opening day."

"Hey, Dory, you don't have to explain to me. If you don't want me in the carousel, that's your business." He smiled wryly, and said, "Not that I think it has anything to do with wet paint. But like I said, that's your business."

He was far too perceptive for her liking. Nervously, she said, "I'm going up to the house to fix lunch. Nothing much, just soup and a sandwich."

"Is that an invitation?"

"Are you hungry?"

"I am."

"Then it is."

He put aside the wire clippers and reached for his jacket, which was hanging from a fence post.

"Do you always do that?" he asked, as they walked back to the house together keeping an uneasy distance between them.

"Do what?"

"Answer a question with a question?"

Dory blushed. "Is that what I did?"

"You're doing it right now."

"And do you always ask so many questions?"

"I'm an inquisitive kind of guy. How about you? Are you as curious as your namesake?"

"My grandfather claims that whenever I do something questionable, I blame it on my curiosity. But have no fear, the gods have left no box for me."

He smiled teasingly as they climbed the steps to the porch. "Ah, but what would you do if they did?"

Dory considered his question, and answered honestly, "Then I suppose I'd have to open it and unleash all that sorrow and mischief upon the world."

Privately, she knew that she had inadvertently opened such a box a long time ago and unleashed upon herself the sorrow of a troubled marriage and its haunting memories.

Ben saw her eyes cloud with sadness and said, "You're forgetting something, aren't you?"

"What's that?"

"The one thing that was left inside the box, and which remains to this day mankind's sole comfort in the face of misfortune. Hope."

Dory paused with her hand on the screen door and looked into Ben's dark eyes, searching for an explanation of why it seemed as if he understood. Not what it was like to make mistakes and suffer the regrets, but what it was like to cling to the one thing that made living with the past possible. The hope that one day everything would be all right.

Chapter 3

"Yes, of course, I understand. Thank you very much, Mr. Evers. Good night."

Dory hung up the phone and returned to the dinner table. "That was Mr. Evers who owns an antique shop in Devil's Corner," she said as she resumed eating.

"Happy-sounding place," Ben remarked.

"It's up in the northern Catskills in Green County," she explained. "By Kaaterskill Falls."

Martin looked up from fussing with Jason and chimed in, "Rip van Winkle country. Filled with dark ravines called cloves after the old Dutch name *kloven*. A darned spooky place, if you ask me."

Jokingly Dory warned, "Careful now, we don't want to scare Ben away after only the first day. We need him around here, there's so much to do."

Her acknowledgment of his worth surprised him, since she had maintained a wary distance all day, sending a polite but cautious signal that friendship was not part of the arrangement. Didn't she realize that her reluctance to be friendly only heightened his interest in knowing her better? He popped a slice of roast potato into his mouth and pondered why it was always the thing one couldn't have that one invariably wanted the most.

"He has a carousel horse for sale," said Dory. "He said he heard from Mr. Meade in Roxbury that I'm looking for one. I'm driving up there next Saturday to look at it. I'd go sooner, but Mr. Evers says he's going fishing next week and won't be back until then."

"What do you need a carousel horse for?" Ben inquired.

The fork slowed to a standstill midway to Dory's mouth at the question that was asked harmlessly enough. "I...we, uh,...we had a fire in the carousel a few years ago." Her gaze came up to chance a swift look at Martin, but he was busy with Jason.

Ben kept right on eating. "Is that why you spend so much time under those tarps?"

She answered carefully, "Yes, it is. I've been restoring the carousel, as you know. Several of the horses were damaged in the fire. A couple were beyond repair. I found one at an auction in Roxbury last autumn and asked Mr. Meade, who runs the local antique shop there, to keep an eye out for me for another one."

"Aren't carousel horses expensive?" he asked.

"They can be, if they're originals from the turn of the century. The one I got at the auction is from the thirties. By then, craftsmanship began to give way to manufacturing. The makers of carousel horses used machines to rough-cut the bodies, although the detail work was still done by hand. It was in pretty bad shape when I got it. I guess nobody thought it was worth restoring, when they can just as easily buy one manufactured using fiberglass shapers and airbrush painters. But the Dutch Mill is one of the few antique carousels left in the country, and I'd like to keep it that way."

Her voice remained level as she spoke, but there was a tenseness in the gentle undertones that did not go unnoticed by Ben. He searched her lovely face in the soft yellow light of the kitchen. What was it, he asked himself, that brought out that ache in her voice? More than anything, he wanted to replace that gloomy look on her face with a smile. She was just so darned pretty when she smiled.

Lifting his glass to her, he said, "My compliments to the cook. This meal is delicious."

"Pop-Pop, look! Mommy's face is all red."

Dory blushed even harder. "Jason, if you're finished eating, why don't you go upstairs and get ready for your bath? I'll be up in a little while."

"Do I have to, Mommy?"

"You know the rules. Bath before bedtime."

"Is Ben gonna have a bath, too?"

"That's up to Ben, isn't it?"

Ben was uncomfortable at being thrust into the midst of their conversation. He was an outsider. He didn't belong there. He couldn't imagine that it would make any difference to anyone what he did. And yet, apparently, it did, for both their faces were turned in his direction, Dory's lovely and Jason's wide-eyed, waiting for his response.

This was new to him. Wanting his own child was one thing. Dealing with this one was another. How was he supposed to be with the kid? Friendly? Aloof?

God knew, with the way things were in the world, they had every reason to mistrust him. And yet they invited him into their home, giving him a glimpse of family life that he never knew existed. Every little exchange, each little interaction hit him hard. Some distant part of his heart longed for the familiarity and the love that filled the kitchen like a warm light.

Jason took a big gulp of milk from his glass and beamed back with a white mustache. "Mommy, can I go with you to that devil's place on Saturday?"

Dory smiled tenderly and leaned over to wipe his face with her napkin. "Don't you have a birthday party to go to on Saturday?"

His face lit up at the reminder. Turning to Ben, he announced, "It's Billy's birthday and there's gonna be a big party."

Ben was reluctant to accept the innocent overtures at friendship, not knowing how to respond. "Sounds great. Can I come?"

"Course not, silly. It's just for kids."

"I guess you're right." Feeling foolish for his effort and eager to make up for it, he said, "Say, how'd you like to help me build an airplane?"

Jason's eyes grew wide. "You can do that? You can build planes?"

"I can build small ones." He held his hands apart. "About so big. I bought a kit in a hobby shop a few weeks ago, and I've been looking for someone just like you to help me build it."

He'd known the instant he saw that P-51 kit in the hobby shop that he had to have it. A crazy thought had flown through his mind that he'd save it for his son and they'd build it together. But hell, he thought as he looked at the boy, that chance might never come, while here was this little guy, filled with enthusiasm and glee over the prospect of building a model plane, reminding Ben a little of himself at that age.

It was easy to get caught up in remembering. Much too easy to let himself imagine that this was the son he was searching for.

"Can I do it, Mommy? Can I help Ben build the plane?"

"I don't know," she hedged.

She wasn't really surprised by Ben's offer. Although he had appeared uneasy, he hadn't complained at all when Jason had returned that afternoon with a cup full of pollywogs, and had insisted that Ben stop what he was doing to look at them. She had attributed Ben's uneasiness to the fact that he probably wasn't around children much. She knew that he was uncomfortable even now, but that he was trying valiantly not to show it.

What was not so easy to determine, however, was the cause of the wince behind his dark eyes whenever he looked at Jason. What painful memories did it evoke for him? He had told her that he had no children, but who knew? Perhaps he'd had one once, and Jason served as a painful reminder of what he had lost. Or maybe he never had a child of his own and secretly longed for one. She'd heard that some men were like that.

Still, it wasn't wise to encourage a friendship between Ben and Jason. After all, Ben would soon be moving on.

"There's so much work to do around here," she said. "I don't know if Ben is going to have much time to build model airplanes."

"Hey," Ben objected, "I get evenings off, don't I?"

"Oh, please, Mommy." Jason begged. "Puleeze."

"I think it would be good for the boy, Dory," Martin put in.

She threw her hands up in mock defense. "All right, all right, you can help Ben build the plane. I can't stand up against the three of you."

Ben's heart gave a little leap of joy at being included. "Great. We can get started on it tonight, right after your bath."

"You promise?"

For a moment Ben indulged in a crazy fantasy as he realized that Jason's dark hair and eyes matched his own. Tracing an *X* over his chest, he said, "Cross my heart."

"Then I'm gonna go take that bath right now!"

In the next instant the fantasy retreated back to reality when the child skipped from the room.

With an incredulous laugh, Dory said, "I've never seen him so eager to take a bath." She got up and began to clear the table.

"Let me give you a hand with that," said Ben, rising to help.

The simple gesture took Dory by surprise and whisked her thoughts far away from the moment.

She was thinking of dinners in the past, when it had been Eddie sitting across from her, and the air in the room had been so thick you could slice it with a knife. Eddie had never offered to help her clear the table, not even at the beginning, before things got bad. Only now, in retrospect, did she realize how much the gesture would have meant to her.

She reached unconsciously for a dinner plate, but

instead of the cool feel of china in her hand, she felt a stab of white lightning when Ben reached for the same plate at that precise moment. His touch was electric, going through her with the unexpected heat of a live wire. For a moment she was incapable of movement, trapped by the current that flowed from his strong fingers into hers. Was it her imagination or did she feel him quiver? It was difficult to tell, her heart was hammering so in her chest.

The plate fell from both their hands and clattered against the table like a giant coin.

Dory pulled her hand back, feeling foolish. This was ridiculous, she chided herself. She had to get control of her emotions if they were going to be sharing a home together for however long Ben decided to stay. She couldn't react like a silly schoolgirl every time their eyes met or their hands chanced to touch.

The last time she had shared her home with a man it had been her husband. Yet here was this stranger sitting in her kitchen, looking almost as if he belonged there, reminding Dory that for too long something had been missing around the house, from the empty seat at the dinner table to the place beside her in bed. How ironic, and secretly exciting, it was to think that she would be living under the same roof with this handsome dark-haired man.

She had to be careful, though, not to react the way she did a few minutes ago when his hand had touched hers. There was no sense encouraging those kinds of feelings, not when she knew, in her heart, that nothing would come of them. She was attracted to him, yes, and granted, they would be sharing a home together, but she had closed the door to romantic involvement a long time ago and wasn't about to open it again.

Dory reached for the plate with trembling fingers, hoping he did not notice the effect he had on her. "That's all right, I'll do this. Why don't you sit down and I'll make some coffee."

It had been a long time since she'd made coffee for anyone other than herself and Martin and the occasional friend who dropped by. But that wasn't a friend, or even an acquaintance, sitting at her kitchen table. It was the stranger with whom she had to share her home. And not just any stranger, but a tall, dark and handsome one whose dark eyes regarded her a little too intently, and at whose touch she was caught like a wildfire out of control. Had he felt her nervousness in the fleeting touch of their fingers? What on earth could he be thinking, sitting there like that, with his lean legs stretched out before him and an unreadable look on his face?

Ben was struggling to regain his composure. His erratic pulse was proof of the chilling effect something so simple as the mere graze of her fingers across his could produce. Yet as he watched her move about the kitchen, there was nothing overtly sexy about her, and he realized that it wasn't lust he was feeling, but something stronger, something much more complicated. More than anything, her lack of pretense or guile was immensely appealing to a man who had learned to trust no one.

The sweet fragrance of Martin's pipe tobacco filled the kitchen, mingling with the aroma of fresh coffee brewing.

Feeling comfortable and strangely at home, Ben said, "When I think of the Catskills, I think of gefilte fish and comedians. I never realized how beautiful it is up here, and so close to Manhattan."

"But that's the problem," Martin complained behind a veil of smoke. "Up here we have some of the best trout streams and prettiest mountains in the whole country, not to mention the art colonies and the ski resorts. Problem is, too many people want a part of it."

Dory set three cups of coffee on the table. "Now you've done it. You've gotten him started."

"Practically everywhere you look," Martin went on, "pastures once filled with holsteins are now dotted with houses built by the flatlanders."

"Sugar?" she asked.

"Three," said Ben.

"Milk?"

"Light."

His coffee was light and sweet, just the way he liked it. From over the rim of his cup he questioned, "What are flatlanders?"

"That's what the native Catskillers call the city folk," Dory explained.

"Second homes, mind you," said Martin, growing more agitated. "When the local folk are losing their first and only homes, those people are building *second* homes."

Dory gave Ben an apologetic look. "The folks in these parts work hard to keep their farms going, often holding two or three jobs to make ends meet. Dairy farms are disappearing at auctions throughout the counties. I was at an auction where a wagon wheel fetched more without the wagon because the bidder, a new arrival to the area, wanted it to decorate his front lawn."

Martin shook his head solemnly. "They took the best farmland in Delaware County."

Dory said with a sigh, "It was bound to happen. A few hundred of us can't sit on all this beautiful land and deprive others."

Ben was struck by her sense of fairness. As much as she might have resented the invasion of the flat-landers, at least she was fair enough to grant them their right to be there. Might she also show the same fairness and understanding for the circumstances surrounding his past? In spite of the spark of hope that ignited inside of him, a voice from the ashes of his past warned him to be careful and not reveal too much about himself.

Dory grew uncomfortable beneath the weight of Ben's dark gaze. He was looking at her in the most curious manner, not in the intimate way that a man looked at a woman, making her cheeks flame with color, but in a searching, questioning way that she sensed had nothing to do with hormones.

She pushed her chair back and rose from the table. "I'd better go help Jason with his bath." With that, she made her escape.

Chapter 4

Once Dory had left the room, Martin tapped the pipe-bowl on his palm and emptied the spent ashes into an ashtray. "That's my cue." Laying down his pipe, he went to the sink where the dishes waited.

"I'll give you a hand with those," Ben offered.

From over his shoulder, Martin replied, "Nonsense. This is my job. If I know Dory, she's had you working your butt off all day. She can be a real taskmaster, that one."

Ben reached for a dish towel and began to dry anyway. "You could've fooled me."

On the contrary, she had a way of requesting in that gentle voice of hers, with a quick unconscious lowering and lifting of her lashes, that made Ben feel instantly like putty in her hands.

"She works pretty hard herself. She spent all day working on the carousel."

Martin shook his head and muttered, "Day after day

she works on that thing, often late into the night, with only the light of the lantern to see by.''

"I offered to help her with it, but she said she could handle it.''

"Dory likes to do things her own way,'' Martin offered. "She's quite an artist. It's amazing what she's done with those horses.''

"I may not be an artist,'' said Ben, "but there must be something I can do to help her.''

Martin rinsed the last dish and turned off the water. "I expect she'll ask for your help when she wants it. Give her some time, my boy. She'll come around.'' He picked up his pipe from the table and left the kitchen.

Ben remained to dry the last of the dishes. Would she? he wondered skeptically. Come around, that is? Judging from her standoffish manner, it didn't seem likely. Meanwhile, the seeds of suspicion about Jason, planted only that afternoon upon learning that the boy was adopted, sprouted like weeds in the hothouse of his mind.

Maybe her desire to maintain a wary distance between them was the best thing. If, by some crazy stroke of luck, Jason did turn out to be his son, it would make taking him away from her that much easier.

Yet as much as Ben wanted to believe that Jason was his son, thinking the physical resemblance between them to be no mere coincidence, he grappled with his conscience over it. He had watched Dory and Jason together during dinner when neither was aware that they were being observed. It was easy to see from the unbounding affection she lavished on the boy that, regardless of who had given birth to Jason, Dory was his mother. How could he even think of taking him away from her? Then again, if Jason was his son, how could he not?

Perhaps it was best to tell her of his suspicion now and get it over with. No matter if he stayed two weeks or two months, he knew that the more he became involved in these people's lives, the harder it would become to keep his suspicions to himself.

He found Martin outside on the porch, sitting in a rocking chair, rocking and smoking his pipe in silence. He sat down on the top step and gazed out into the surrounding darkness for many long minutes without speaking. The trees stood like sentries in the darkness. Through them he could make out the carousel, a pale and ghostly image against the night.

Martin's voice broke the evening stillness in a low, reminiscing tone. "I was born right here in Delaware County, raised in the company of foxes and owls. Used to have a farm in the old days. Nothing much. A few head of dairy cows and some corn. Enough to keep us going. It's difficult land. With each frost and thaw that old earth heaves up a new crop of stones that have to be cleared before spring plowing can begin. We call it picking rock." He drew on his pipe and let the smoke out slowly through pursed lips to disperse into the evening breeze.

"Sounds like hard work," said Ben from the moonlit shadows.

"Harder than most, not as hard as some. Planting in spring, haying in summer, harvesting the corn in fall. Winter was the time for fixing the machinery. Sometimes I can still feel the flanks of the cows warming my cheek on those cold, dark winter mornings when I did the milking. There's a rhythm to farming that gets in your blood and stays there no matter what else you might do in life.''

"How'd you go from farming to running an amusement park?''

"The bank took the farm in the late fifties. By then, my wife was gone. My son and daughter-in-law had everything invested in this place, so I came here to live with them.'' A shadow crossed his face in the moonlight. "We lost them both in a car accident about twelve years ago. After that it was just Dory and me running the place.''

There was something about the way the old man spoke fondly of his past despite its hardships and tragedies that made Ben envious. Here was a man who had found serenity in his life, something Ben longed for after years of turmoil and disillusionment in his own life.

"What about Dory's husband?''

Martin gave a slow, sad shake of the head. "Eddie wasn't suited for it. Then came the trouble, and...'' His words trailed off into awkward silence.

Ben didn't press the issue. He knew firsthand how painful some memories could be.

"I hear the fishing is pretty good in these parts.''

"That would be the Beaver Kill and Willowemoc,'' Martin eagerly replied. "Two of the best trout streams in the East. Say, do you fish?''

He'd spent a lot of time in prison thinking about the small, everyday things he swore he would savor if he ever got the chance. "It's something I always wanted to do but just never found the time for. I'd love to give it a try, though. What do you use? Worms?'' The prospect delighted him.

"Usually. But take it from an old trout fisherman,

my boy. There's one thing you must always put on your hook, and that's your heart.''

There was something warm and comfortable and immensely appealing to Ben about the joy Martin derived from the simple pleasures of life—a joy Ben found himself yearning to know. He laughed softly. "I'll keep that in mind."

"I've been teaching Jason how to fly-fish," said Martin. "By the way, that was a nice thing you did, offering to let the boy help you build the plane. He doesn't get much opportunity to be with a man young enough to be his father. All he has is me, and I'm old."

It was the first time Ben had ever heard anyone refer to him as being a father, or anything even remotely like it, and it shook him to his core. Was it possible? Could he really be? A father, that is, to some little boy, maybe even to Jason?

"It appears Jason's taken a natural liking to you," said Martin, unwittingly complicating the issue. "I don't know when I've ever seen him so friendly. Usually he's kind of shy around strangers."

But maybe they weren't strangers, Ben caught himself thinking. Maybe the same blood coursed through their veins. How likely was it that Jason would take to him so easily if what Martin said about him being shy around strangers was true? Could it be that, like him, the boy sensed something that went beyond understanding or explanation? Either way, it was a compelling indication of something Ben had only just imagined. Suddenly his uneasiness and uncertainty over what being a father was all about was lessened. The little boy, in his friendly eagerness to reach out to Ben, had inadvertently provided him with some answers.

Ben's voice issued from the moonlit shadows. "What happened to Dory's husband?"

Martin answered with a sigh, "He died."

Ben was about to inquire into the cause of Eddie McBride's death, when the screen door creaked behind him. Turning his head, he saw Dory standing in the doorway.

Silhouetted against the glow of light that came from inside the house, she was like a vision out of a dream, soft curves all warm and inviting. Her beauty appealed to him in the most primal of ways, and he longed to bury himself in her soft womanly warmth. But there was more to her appeal than just a pretty face. She was like a doe in the woods, skittish, wary, vulnerable, pushing his basic instincts to something far more dangerous. It had to do with this crazy feeling he had to protect her, to wrap his arms around her and tell her that everything would be all right, even though he knew from personal experience that it wasn't always true.

She touched him in a way no woman had before. In only a day, without even trying, she had pierced his resolve never to need or want another human being again. Somehow, she had managed to give him a reason to get up in the morning, if for no other reason, than to see her lovely face and to feel the awakening of something deep inside that he thought had died in him a long time ago.

It was just his cursed luck that he would feel such instant attraction to this woman, for it only complicated an already painful dilemma. How could he tell her that he thought Jason might be his son without proof to substantiate such an outrageous claim? A birth certificate wouldn't necessarily prove anything. Allison had perjured herself on the witness stand to keep him from getting his son. Who's to say she didn't just as easily lie about the name of the father on the birth certificate? Without proof, what could he do? He couldn't very well walk up to Dory and say, "I think you're the most beautiful woman I've ever seen and I long for you. And oh, by the way, I think Jason is my son and I want to take him away from you."

She came to sit beside him on the top step of the porch. Her voice was soft against the night.

"Jason's putting on his pajamas. If you're too tired to start that plane tonight, I could just tell him that—"

"No way," he said, rising to his feet. "A promise is a promise."

She looked up at the tall figure that towered over her and smiled, a rare and beautiful smile that stole his breath away.

"Thanks. It's all he talked about during his bath. There's something else you can do, if you don't mind. I'd appreciate it if you would drive with me to Devil's Corner on Saturday. If that horse is any good and I do buy it, I'll need help getting it home. If you're still around by then, that is."

Oh, he'd be around. He had decided that the instant he learned that Jason was adopted. He shot a quick glance at Martin, who'd been right after all when he said that Dory would ask for his help if she needed it.

"Sure, Dory, I'll go with you."

The steady creaking of the rocking chair ceased.

Dory aimed a look at Martin, and warned, "Not a word out of you."

He gave her an innocent look as he leaned forward to empty his pipebowl.

"I'm going inside to pay some bills and see if I can't get that checkbook balanced," she said.

The aroma of dinner still hung in the kitchen as Dory sat hunched over the table trying to get in order a checkbook that defied balancing. Martin's haphazard record keeping made it a difficult task. Two hours later, satisfied that a difference of a few cents didn't matter, she pushed herself away from the table and went upstairs. On her way to her room, she paused to peek into Ben's room through the door that was left partly ajar.

Ben and Jason were sitting on the floor at the foot of the bed, studying the plans that were spread out over the hardwood planks.

"There, see that?" said Ben. He pointed to a figure drawn on the paper. "See if you can find that piece for me in the box."

Jason bit his lip and scrutinized the balsa pieces. "Here it is," he said excitedly. "I found it."

He dropped it into Ben's big palm. "Is that it, Ben? Is that the right one?"

"It sure is, champ. Now I want you to watch how it's done. Then I want you to try the next one."

"Me? Oh, wow!"

Ben could still recall the excitement he had felt the first time his father had let him help build something around the house. It had been a counter in the garage, just a simple, flat counter made of plain old plywood, but how excited he'd been to hand his father the nails one by one as if it were the most important part of the job. He could see the same emotion on Jason's face, along with that eerie resemblance that defied coincidence.

An evening breeze came into the room, billowing the curtains, as Ben pondered again the crazy possibility that Jason was his son. Why not? he reasoned. His son would be just about Jason's age. And he felt something special for this little boy, something that went beyond the simple tenderness one might feel for someone else's child. With his impish ways, Jason was delving deeper into his aching heart. Jason, who might be the son he was searching for, the one piece of himself that was left in the wreckage of his life.

With Jason chattering away, they were blissfully unaware of the figure that watched from the doorway, until she pushed the door open and entered the room.

"How's it going, you two?"

Ben looked up and smiled. "Great. It looks like we've got a future aeronautical designer here."

Realizing what he'd said, his smile quickly vanished. We? he questioned, aghast. Dear God, was he already beginning to think of Jason as his?

"Mommy, Ben says it's gonna take weeks to finish the plane."

"Considering the progress you've made in the last two hours, I can see that."

"Ah, but that's the joy of it," said Ben. "You never want it to end. It's like reading a good book." Or like what he imagined making love to her must be like, he added privately.

"Well, right now, Jason, it's time for bed."

"Aw, I don't want to go to bed," the boy whined.

"Hey, pal, you heard what your mother said. Go on, off to bed with you. The plane will be here tomorrow."

"Oh, okay."

Dory was waiting for him by the door. "Come on, I'll tuck you in."

Jason tugged on Dory's sleeve and crooked his finger for her to come closer. Bending, she listened to his whisper at her ear.

"Are you sure?" she asked him.

He nodded solemnly.

"Well, I don't know, but you can go ahead and ask."

Jason buried his face in the side of her leg, turning suddenly shy. "You ask him, Mommy."

She shrugged, and half-apologetically said to Ben, "He'd like you to tuck him in. But if you're too tired—"

Ben rose fluidly from the floor and came forward, a look of mild astonishment on his handsome face. "No problem. If it's okay with you, I'd be happy to."

She could have no idea what Jason's innocent request meant to him. In fact, as he walked down the hallway toward Jason's room, even he wasn't sure he knew what it meant to him. Until he felt a small hand wiggle into his, and suddenly, it seemed like the most natural thing in the world to be walking down the hallway hand in hand with the boy.

He was touched by the way Jason peered up at him and asked, "Will you read me a story?"

And jolted by the sound of his own deep voice in reply. "I'll do better than that. I'll *tell* you a story."

When Jason was all tucked in, Dory ran her hand gently across his cheek and swept a rebellious dark curl from his brow. Bending to give him a kiss, she whispered, "Sweet dreams, my precious boy. I love you."

A little voice replied, "I love you, too, Mommy."

"I'll send Pop-Pop up to say good-night."

Turning to Ben she whispered, "He'll be out like a light before you even finish."

She paused at the door to look back at the two of them, trying to reconcile the unwelcome feelings she had for Ben Stone with the warm emotions that came from watching him with her son.

The edge of the bed sagged from Ben's weight when he sat down on it, and said, "Okay, this one's about a cat named Priscilla and a rabbit named Bunky who live in the back of a little country restaurant."

It was the very pair he had spied one day while eating breakfast at one of the inns he had stopped at along the road. The owner had scooted them away with a broom, calling them by their names as they took cover. Funny, how the memory came back to him like that, as if it had been lurking in his subconscious for weeks, waiting for just the right occasion to make an appearance. And judging from the smile on Jason's face, the timing couldn't have been better.

Making up a story about a rabbit and a cat wasn't so difficult after all. The adventures he sent them on delighted not only Jason, who listened raptly between yawns, but himself as well, for his newly found flair for telling bedtime stories.

Martin came in to say good-night and stayed for a while to listen to the story.

When Jason was sound asleep, they tiptoed from the room.

"Good job," Martin whispered. He left Jason's door slightly open to a sliver of light from the hallway, explaining as they walked toward the stairs, "Sometimes he's afraid of the dark."

"I know," said Ben.

Martin look at him questioningly.

"What I mean is…" He realized too late how his impulsive remark must have sounded. How could he explain the similarities he saw between Jason and himself without arousing the old man's suspicion? "I was like that too as a kid." He laughed nervously. "Most kids are afraid of the dark, aren't they?"

"I suppose. Although Dory wasn't. As a kid, she wasn't afraid of anything. I'd catch her sometimes climbing out of her bedroom window, using the wisteria vine like she was the queen of the jungle. Or swimming in the creek, holding her breath longer than any of the other kids, staying under until she had you wading frantically out there after her, only to pop up laughing hysterically. Do you know, one time she even backed down a bulldog? Fearless, she was. And then…" His words trailed off into silence. When he spoke again, it was in a voice dim with regret. "She grew up, I guess."

Downstairs, Martin pulled a white crocheted sweater from the hall closet. "She's out there working. I was going to bring her this, but there's a show I want to catch on the TV. Would you mind doing it for me?"

Moonlight fell in patches through the branches of the trees as Ben made his way down the narrow path that led to the carousel. He could see her shadow moving against the tarpaulin that glowed in the darkness.

Habit had made Dory pick the safest spot to place the lantern, where it was not likely to fall over and cause history to painfully repeat itself.

Tonight as she worked among the horses by lanternlight, she felt none of the remorse that generally accompanied her silent hours of solitude. Her heart felt surprisingly lighter than it had in a long time, as if there were no memories to weigh it down. She was even amused to hear herself humming a little tune in time to the confident strokes of the paintbrush.

She told herself she was happy because her work on the carousel was coming along so well, but in her heart she knew it was because of a pair of dark eyes, a smile that threatened to melt even her fearful heart, and a masculine nature that was strong enough to be tender to a child.

The sound of her name called quietly against the night, silenced her humming and stilled her movements for several moments, before she rose gracefully.

She swept aside a corner of the tarpaulin and stood on the edge of the carousel, gazing out at him.

"I just wanted you to know that he's asleep," he said.

Dory was grateful for the darkness that concealed the blush of embarrassment on her cheeks at having been caught thinking about him.

"Thank you. That was a nice thing you did."

"It was my pleasure." And his pain, he added silently. "Martin asked me to bring you this. Is there anything else I can do for you before I go in?"

She said nothing to him about it being her good sweater, one that Martin knew very well she would never wear while working on the carousel. She reached down and took it from his outstretched hand.

"No. I'm finished here for tonight. But if you wait, I'll put the lantern out and walk back with you."

While Dory finished up, Ben waited patiently outside, listening to the crickets chirping beneath leaves. He was curious about what she did in there hour upon hour, but three long years in prison had taught him to value his own privacy above all else, and he wouldn't invade hers. He didn't know the cause of her sadness, either, or why she felt compelled to keep him at such a distance. He knew only that, little by little, he found himself wanting her.

The light inside the carousel went out, plunging the surroundings into blackness.

"I'll leave the lantern here," said Dory. "We can see our way back by moonlight."

In the darkness of the carousel, however, she did not see the tarpaulin gathered around her foot. She knew she was caught in it only when she attempted to step forward and felt herself falling.

She gave a small cry as her arms flew out to her sides for balance. If Ben hadn't reacted in a heartbeat, she would have fallen off the carousel right onto her face. As it was, she fell forward straight into his arms, hard up against his chest.

The breath went out of him when he caught her, not from the impact of her fall, but from the effect of having her suddenly so close. Later there would be time for reproaches. For now, there was only the urgent awareness of having her in his arms, of looking into her eyes for several stunned moments, of feeling the warmth of her body against him.

In the deep green depths of her eyes he thought he saw her beckon. His logic drowned in a sea of emotion as his arms tightened around her and his lips came down over hers.

His kiss was soft and tentative, lips moving over hers, exploring the texture and the taste of her. A distant part of him remembered what it was like to kiss a woman, even though he knew it had never been like this, so tender and achingly necessary.

Her soft tongue met his halfway in a discovery that left him breathless. Its tentative probing left little doubt that she was as scared as he was.

Dory moved instinctively into Ben's embrace. It had been such a long time since she'd been held in a man's arms. Such a long time since she'd been kissed. And never like this, with such hunger and regret. But the regret was as much hers as it was his. How could she let this happen? Shocked at the ease with which she had succumbed to her own desire to be kissed, she pushed herself away from him.

There was an expression of relief on his handsome face when he released her and stepped back.

"Dory, I—"

She put her hand up to staunch whatever apology he was about to make. It was bad enough that she had gone against her own better judgment for one precarious moment. Did she have to hear him apologize for going against his? She hurried off down the path, leaving him standing in the mottled moonlight.

Ben told himself that he had reacted the way any man would if a beautiful woman fell into his arms. In fact, it wasn't even his own reaction that surprised him the most. It was Dory's. Was it his imagination, or had she actually pressed herself closer to him? He hadn't expected her to kiss him back, but she had, and every fiber of his being told him she had liked it as much as he had.

But it was more than just a kiss between strangers beside a carousel that satisfied some foolish longing inside of him. It was about how she had stirred his coffee to the desired sweetness earlier. It was about possibly having found his son and being, temporarily at least, a part of Dory's family. Even though he had to admit he liked being the man around the house, he'd be a fool to think it went any further than sharing their home for the time being.

Now, having kissed her, he wasn't sure if it would be harder for him to tell her about Jason, or easier. Had he ruined his chances of getting his son back, or was the way now clear? He needed time, not just to get to know Jason better, but to get to know Dory, to see if it was possible to win her over to his side so that she would help him uncover the truth of whether or not he was Jason's father.

The uncertainty of it followed him even into his dreams, as he tossed and turned later that night, unable to find solace in slumber.

Just down the hallway, Dory, too, was having trouble sleeping, plagued by the thought of Ben's kiss and the eagerness with which she had responded to it.

She must have dozed off, and had no idea how long she'd been asleep when she awoke with a start. The sheet was twisted about her slender legs and her skin was dotted with perspiration, yet it wasn't a fitful dream that had awakened her. She lay there for several moments, listening to the silence of the night. Outside everything was still. No breeze blew. Not even a cricket chirped.

She turned her head on the pillow and sought out the clock on the night table beside the bed. The LED display glowed like a tiny read beacon through the darkness. It read one-thirty. She closed her eyes and tried to slip back into sleep, when she heard a sound that made every nerve in her body snap to attention.

With a start she realized it had been Jason, crying out in the dead of the night, that had awakened her.

She was in motion even as the realization took shape in her brain.

In her bare feet she hurried down the hall toward Jason's room.

She routinely left Jason's bedroom door ajar so that the soft yellow glow of the hall light that she left on for him each night would provide enough gentle illumination to ease his fear of the dark. The first thing she noticed, however, was that the door was fully open, pushed back up against the wall as if someone had done it in a hurry.

Martin, she thought. But that wasn't Martin's shadowy figure hovering over Jason's bed. It was Ben who had gotten there before her.

For several seconds she stood frozen in the doorway. Her first impulse was to rush in to protect her son, but the deep cadence of Ben's voice told her that there was no threat to Jason from him.

"The closet. The closet."

Jason's little voice called anxiously from beneath the sheet that was pulled up to just below a pair of frightened eyes.

Ben went to the closet, stood before the door, and said threateningly, "Okay, you monsters, if you're in there, you'd better get out now."

He grasped the knob and yanked the closet door open. When the supposed monsters didn't jump out, he poked his head inside and looked all around. "Nope," he concluded, "no monsters in here."

"Under the bed," Jason cried. "Check under the bed."

Ben got down on his hands and knees and peered into the darkness under the child's bed. "No monsters here, either."

"M-maybe they jumped out the window."

"Tell you what," Ben said as he strode to the window. "Why don't I close this for tonight?" It was worth it, he reasoned, to sacrifice a little fresh air in order to soothe the kid's fears.

"I checked everywhere. I guess you're right. They must have slipped out through the window."

"Did you lock it tight?" the little voice inquired.

"Don't worry. They won't be back. Do you think you can get some sleep now?"

Slowly, the sheet came back down and settled beneath Jason's chin. "I guess so."

"Okay, cowboy, why don't you close your eyes and give it a try."

The boy's eyes closed obediently.

Ben remained at the side of the bed looking down at the face which only minutes ago had been wide-eyed with fright. It wasn't until he heard the child's steady breathing and knew he was sleeping that he stepped away from the bed.

He met Dory outside in the hallway. There was a strange look on her face.

In a hushed voice so as not to awaken the child, he said quickly, "I hope you don't mind. I heard him cry out and I thought...I didn't mean to interfere."

He was barechested and barefooted, dressed only in his jeans, which he had obviously pulled on in a hurry without bothering to zip them. A line of softly curled dark hair ran down his belly and disappeared into the vee formed by the open zipper. With the heat of his kiss still fresh in her mind, it was the last thing Dory needed to see.

She wasn't thinking of the sight she presented to him, dressed only in a sheer white nightgown, her exposed flesh looking translucent in the glow of the night-light outside Jason's room, until she saw his gaze drop, and felt suddenly naked beneath his stare.

She used the opportunity of the sleeping child to keep her voice to a whisper, hiding her nervousness. "That's all right. I saw what you did, and I'm grateful to you for it."

They turned and started back down the hallway toward their rooms.

"I hope I did okay in there," said Ben. "I'm new at that sort of thing."

"You did just fine," she assured him.

"Is that what you do? Check the closets and under the bed?"

"I usually just try to soothe him and coax him back to sleep by reassuring him that the monsters aren't real."

"Oh, great," he responded with a groan. "And I told him they escaped through the window."

"That's okay. Really. I was surprised that he fell back to sleep so easily. It usually takes me a while to convince him that he's safe. It makes perfect sense. Those monsters are real to him. By acknowledging them and locking the window so they can't get back in, you gave him something he can deal with. That's why he so readily believed you when you told him they were gone."

Half to himself, he said, "If only we could make our own monsters disappear so easily."

Dory looked up at him, her eyes widening with surprise. It was as if he had found a way into her thoughts and read each one.

"The trick," she said, "is learning to live with them."

"Is that what you do?" he asked. He didn't know what demons haunted Dory, but he had sensed their presence since the moment he met her.

She lifted her bare shoulders in a little shrug, and said, "I try."

"What is it that causes you to try so hard?"

"Is it that obvious?"

"Only to someone else who's trying just as hard."

She hadn't answered his question, but as far as he was concerned, that was all right. For in acknowledging that she tried to live with her demons, she had given him the first indication that there was a reason for the sadness he saw in her eyes. It made him feel just a little bit closer to her.

At the door to her room Dory paused to look at him. "Thanks, Ben. I appreciate what you did." She regarded him thoughtfully for a moment. "You'd make a good father." She closed the door softly behind her, with a whispered "good night."

Father. The emotional impact of that word rooted Ben to his spot. He had begun his quest to find his son, without ever really thinking about what it meant emotionally to be a father. He'd thought of the things they would do together, like playing catch and building model airplanes. He'd imagined the talks they might one day have, of girls and cars and baseball's current MVP. But he had never considered the feelings that would come with parenthood, until he watched Dory and Jason together, and saw their openness toward one another, and realized that in order to be a father, he would have to open himself up, and risk being hurt, much more than he wanted to.

He started back to his room, not knowing what he

was getting himself into, feeling strangely hopeful, and yet, at the same time, wondering if he had a right to feel any hope at all.

Chapter 5

Dory carefully removed the strips of bacon sizzling in the pan and laid them out on a paper towel.

"I told you," she said gently from over her shoulder, "you can't go with me and Ben on Saturday because you'll be at Billy's birthday party."

Jason was seated at the kitchen table, frowning into his bowl of cereal. "But I don't want to go to Billy's stupid birthday party."

"I'll bet you won't think it's so stupid once you're there."

"I know, but—"

"And besides, you know that long rides make you carsick."

But not even the prospect of stopping several times along the way to be sick could deter a little boy whose mind was made up.

"I won't get sick this time, Mommy, I promise."

Dory looked over her shoulder at her son, and questioned, "Why this sudden interest in coming with me?"

His small shoulders lifted with an exaggerated gesture.

"Oh, but I think you *do* know," she countered. "Can it have anything to do with Ben?" She had not failed to notice the way he raced to wherever Ben happened to be each day after Martin picked him up from day care. She had her answer when his face broke into a grin so precious it stole her heart away. "You like Ben, don't you?"

"He's letting me help build the plane," he said proudly.

"Is that the only reason you like him?"

Jason screwed up his face in thought. "He lets me use the hammer, and the screwdriver, too. And yesterday he put me up on his shoulders and I could see real far."

Thinking back, Dory could not remember a single time she had seen Eddie lift Jason onto his shoulders. And Martin's arthritis wouldn't allow it. Surprisingly, it was the first time Jason had ridden on a man's shoulders. How many other things, she wondered sadly, was her son deprived of because she hadn't been able to make a go of her marriage?

Feeling the old, familiar sting of blame, she placed two slices of bread in the toaster and said, "I'm glad you like Ben."

"Do *you*, Mommy? Do you like Ben, too?"

The question took Dory by surprise, not so much because it was a difficult question to answer, but because she didn't know the answer. How could she explain sexual attraction to a not-quite-five-year-old? He was far too young to understand the fear she had of getting involved, when in his own innocent enthusiasm, he wanted nothing more than to dive in deeper.

As it had a hundred times since that night, her mind wandered back to the kiss outside the carousel. She hoped she hadn't given Ben the wrong impression. It had happened so unexpectedly that she had reacted before she could stop herself. In moments she'd been consumed by a heat from within that had threatened to scorch her very soul. It had left her weak and uncertain and wanting more.

He had kissed her hungrily, exploringly, the warmth of his body pressed to hers burning through her clothes, past her skin, setting her on fire inside. Her cheeks reddened at the thought of how she had responded. Trapped in his arms, she had wanted his strength, not just the muscles, but the inner strength that she had sensed in him from the beginning. There had been no words, only needs, and feelings stronger than any she had felt in a very long time. It had both excited her and frightened her. If his kiss alone had the power to do that to her, what would it be like to make love with him? Surely, that was something she would never find out.

She turned back to the eggs in the bowl and proceeded to scramble them. Hesitantly, but honestly, she answered, "Yes, Jason, I like Ben, too."

"Great. Then I can go with you on Saturday."

It wasn't that she didn't want Jason to spend time with Ben. In the two weeks since Ben had been there, it was easy to see that Jason lit up in his presence. But why give him the false impression that the relationship meant anything when soon Ben would be gone, and Jason would be one disappointed little boy. It broke Dory's heart. She wished there were some way she could shield her son from the hurt he would undoubtedly feel and not understand.

The funny thing was, something told her that she, too, would be hurt by Ben's leaving, and that understanding would not diminish the pain. But then, she was used to people leaving, in one way or another.

"You'll see, Mommy, I won't get carsick. It'll work out."

Her son's eager voice brought Dory back to the matter at hand. She wanted to tell him that things didn't always work out, that life wasn't always fair, and that by Saturday, the excitement of Billy's birthday party would far outweigh a ride to Devil's Corner with her and Ben. But as she buttered the toast, she said, "If you don't hurry up and finish your breakfast, you won't be ready when Pop-Pop comes down to drive you to Mrs. Norton's."

Mrs. Norton ran the day-care center in the nearby town of Libertyville. Having once been Dory's own third-grade teacher, Dory felt secure in the knowledge that Jason would receive the benefit of Mrs. Norton's stern, but loving, care.

"Come on," she gently coaxed, "eat just a little bit more, then drink your milk and you're finished."

When the predictable protest did not come, she turned from the stove and saw what had silenced him, the tall figure standing in the doorway, seeming to take up the entire space with his masculine form.

She had no idea how long he'd been standing there, or how much of their conversation he'd overheard. Had he heard the part where she said she liked him? Her pulse revved, and she could feel the hot flame of embarrassment rise to her cheeks.

"Good morning."

His voice was mellow and smooth, giving no indication that he'd heard anything. Yet it was also lacking the friendliness she had come to recognize these past couple of weeks. At times she cringed for him when he tried to be friendly in spite of her resistance. This morning, however, it was absent, and Dory was surprised to find herself disappointed. She reached for a plate, praying he didn't notice her feelings.

"Good morning," she said pleasantly. "Have a seat. Breakfast is almost ready."

By silent, mutual consent, the subject of the kiss had never been mentioned since that first night, although the remembrance of it was strung like barbed wire between them.

"Hey, pal," Ben said to the boy as he took his seat at the table, "that cereal looks mighty good. Did you leave any for me?"

Dory recognized it as a ploy to get Jason to eat his cereal. Oh God, she groaned to herself as she prepared Ben's plate, he *had* heard their conversation.

Jason began to gobble up his cereal as if on cue. "Uh-uh," he managed as he downed spoonfuls. With a final full mouth he held up an empty bowl and proclaimed, "Not a drop."

Dory caught Ben's eyes and gave him a little smile of thanks as she placed a plate of scrambled eggs, bacon and buttered toast before him. Without asking, she stirred three teaspoons of sugar into a mug of coffee and set it down on the table.

"Smells great," said Ben. "How about you? Aren't you eating?"

"I had breakfast over an hour ago. I'm on my second cup of coffee now, but that should do it. Too much caffeine makes me jittery. I've got some detail work to do today, and I need a steady hand."

"I thought I'd paint some of the games today," he said. "How does Day-Glo sound to you?"

"Bright."

"That's what this place needs. Hot colors appeal to the young. I'm telling you, Dory, your business will double. Trust me on this." His eye for detail and color had made him very successful in his former profession, but she didn't know that.

Something about Ben's confident attitude made Dory trust his judgment. Maybe it was the forthright manner in which he looked at her as he spoke, as if he knew what he was talking about. And why not? For mingled with the unexplained hurt she saw now and then in his eyes was a fierce intelligence. She didn't know what he had once been, or what had led a man like him to such a haphazard existence. She knew only that she trusted him.

Still, she hedged, not wishing to disrupt the secure feeling she got from the familiar old surroundings by changing them so radically. "The Dutch Mill has always been the way it is, and we've done all right."

"What have you go to lose? If you don't like the way they look, I'll paint them back to the way they are now."

"We don't have enough time left to waste it on repainting."

"I'll make the time."

She sensed that he wasn't being obstinate as he sat there eating his breakfast, only logical. It wasn't that the games could not stand a new coat of paint, and Day-Glo wasn't really the issue. When had he begun to take things into his own hands? To make his own decisions on what needed to be done? And when, to her chagrin, did she begin liking it?

"All right. But if I don't like it—"

"Back it goes," he interjected.

"Back what goes?" Martin questioned upon entering the room.

"Ben is going to paint some of the games today," Dory said, a note of skepticism in her tone. "He can tell you what he needs, and maybe you can pick it up after you drop off Jason."

"Absolutely. What'll it be, my boy?"

As Ben ticked off the type and colors of paint he wanted, his gaze strayed to the counter where Dory was packing Jason's lunch. From behind she was a symmetrical form with one line curving gracefully into another, creating the swells and hollows that made a man hunger, even when his belly was full from breakfast. Through her jeans he could see the faint outline of her panties. He smiled appreciatively, and wondered whether women knew how sexy panty lines were to a man.

That she wasn't wearing a bra was evident in the way her breasts pressed against the soft flannel of her shirt as she moved about the kitchen. Yet as much as he wanted to cup the warm fullness of them in his palms, he resisted the thought with the same kind of fierceness of will that had gotten him through three years in prison. A kiss was one thing, but he couldn't risk getting involved with her, not when he held the power to break her heart by taking her son away from her.

As he had stood in the doorway observing both mother and child, he'd seen the bond between them that would not be easily broken, and he had known then that this was the day he would tell her.

"Okay, got it." Into his pocket Martin stuffed the paper upon which he had scribbled Ben's order.

Even his aging eyes could not help but notice the glow on Dory's cheeks this morning that reminded him of the Dory he used to know. For too long there had been a melancholy ring to her laughter, and her loneliness showed in her eyes. Yet his every attempt to encourage her to date was met with a smile and the same sweet proclamation. "I have you, and Jason, and the Dutch Mill," she would say. "Who needs more than that?"

Yet it was obvious by the color that tinted her cheeks, and by the way she kept her eyes shyly averted, that she was aware of the dark gaze that followed her every move, and Martin wondered if her question wasn't already answered.

He cleared his throat and said, "Where's that boy? It's time we got going."

Jason raced into the room from wherever he had disappeared to. "Here I am, Pop-Pop."

Dory handed him his lunchbox, then bundled him up in her arms and gave him a big hug. "Have fun today. And remember, Mommy loves you."

She gave Martin a kiss on his seamed cheek and sent the two of them off together.

The tender scene filled Ben with longing, pushing his emotions beyond the breaking point. His fingers rapped nervously on the knotty pine of the kitchen table as he watched them say their goodbyes. He knew he had to tell her. Yet he also knew that doing so would destroy any possibility, however remote, of ever becoming a part of the family scene he witnessed each morning.

"Want more?"

Her voice was tentative, a little husky, and unerringly beautiful with its soft, sexy tone. Yet it failed to put Ben at ease in view of what he knew he must do.

"Coffee?" she prompted, when she received no response from him.

"No, thank you."

"That was nifty work you did getting Jason to eat his breakfast. You're a natural. It's too bad you don't have children of your own."

She hadn't intended it as anything other than simple flattery, but when she saw the wince in his eyes, she knew he had taken it for more than that. "What I mean is—"

Ben spoke up quickly. "It was nothing. It always worked on me when I was a kid, so I figured I'd give it a try."

"So, had you been standing there long?"

"Long enough to know he didn't want to eat. Why was he being difficult?"

"He wants to drive with us to Devil's Corner on Saturday."

"It's okay with me, if it's okay with you," he offered.

"Take my word for it," she said confidently, "come Saturday morning, the only thing you'll hear Jason talking about is the birthday party. We'll drop him off on our way, and I can guarantee he won't even look back."

He envied her for how well she knew her son. Wishing for the same kind of familiarity, he said, "There's something I've been wanting to speak to you about."

"You're not thinking of painting everything Day-Glo, are you?" she said jokingly.

"Not unless you want me to. No, actually I wanted to speak to you about Jason."

"Has he been taking up too much of your time? I'll have a talk with him. Jason is just a very inquisitive child."

"Yes, I know." Much as he himself was at that age, he remembered. One more similar trait between them. Was it his imagination, or was he seeing more and more similar traits every day?

"He told me you let him use your tools, and that you put him up on your shoulders. I can't tell you what that means to him."

"You don't have to. I saw the look of pure joy on his face. And no, he hasn't been taking up too much of my time. It's easy to see he misses the influence of a father in his life." He chanced a look at her and saw a shadow of unexplained regret wash across her face. This wasn't going to be easy.

"I was wondering about the boy's father. Not your late husband, but, you know, the biological father. What do you suppose he was like?"

"Beats me," said Dory. "Every time I see something new in Jason I wonder if it's because he's simply who he is, or whether it's something he's inherited from his birth parents." She lowered her eyes and said, "I like to think there's some of me in him, too."

"Do you think you would ever let him meet his birth father?"

"I've given that a lot of thought. I suppose if the day comes when Jason wants to meet his father, I'll do whatever I can to help him find him." She paused, and added, "And to prepare him for the possibility that his father might not want to meet him."

To a man desperate to find his son, it was inconceivable to Ben that any father in similar circumstance would not want to be united with his son.

"What if his biological father wanted to find him? Would you be willing to do whatever was necessary to help?"

"I don't know. Why do you ask?"

Ben hesitated. The words he had rehearsed a thousand times in his head would not emerge. "I—I gave a child up for adoption once, and I often think about one day finding him." It was not a lie, yet neither was it entirely the truth.

Sudden understanding brightened her eyes. "That would explain it, then, that look I see on your face sometimes when you're with Jason. Ben, I'm so sorry. I had no idea."

In prison he had perfected the art of letting no one read his expression, for fear of knowing his thoughts. What little privacy there was was to be found inside his own head. Whoever would have guessed that this slender, soft-spoken woman would do what the toughest convict or prison guard could not do, see past his facade all the way to the tender ache beneath?

He asked, "Is it that obvious?"

She didn't want to admit that it was only obvious to someone who was staring as intently as she sometimes did, so she waved off his concern, saying, "Haven't you ever heard of a woman's intuition, or a mother's wisdom?" She sat down beside him at the table. "There are organizations that can help you. I have the name of one written down somewhere."

He kept his gaze averted to the grainy surface of

the table, unable to look at her. "That may not be necessary. I think I know where my son is."

"At least that's a start. Maybe you can hire an attorney and see about some kind of visitation rights."

"What do you think they'd do, the adoptive parents?"

"That's hard to say. All you can do is hope they understand your need to be a part of your son's life."

His eyes came up slowly to meet hers. "What would *you* do?"

"You mean if I were you?"

"No. I mean if you were the adoptive parent and I showed up to claim your son...my son?"

Dory felt a sudden tensing of her muscles. She didn't like the route his questions were taking. "I—I don't know."

"Would you understand, Dory? Would you understand my need to be a part of my son's life?"

"Why are you asking me this? I told you, I don't know. How can I say how I would feel? You're talking about a mother somewhere who faces the very real possibility of sharing her child with you. In my case, we're talking hypothetically, aren't we?"

There was no answer, only a look in his eyes that seemed to beg forgiveness.

"Ben? Aren't we?"

"Dory, there's something I have to tell you. It's been driving me crazy since the day I got here."

She wasn't aware of rising from the table and backing away, or of shaking her head slowly, incredulously, from side to side as a terrible connection began to take shape.

"Wh-what is it?" She could hear the tremor of fear rising in her voice and fought to keep it under control.

Ben's face was a tangle of emotions as he struggled for the words. There was no easy way to do it, so he pulled in a deep, galvanizing breath and said, "I have reason to think that Jason is my son."

The words, though barely uttered, ricocheted off the walls of Dory's mind like gunshots fired at close range.

"Y-you don't know what you're saying. What on earth makes you think such a thing?"

The initial fear his insane declaration inspired gave way rapidly to anger as Dory's maternal instincts came rushing to the surface, and her expression changed from vulnerable to belligerent in a matter of seconds.

Ben had steeled himself as best he could against the tears that he was sure would come with the news. But this was not the teary-eyed response he had expected. This was the full-blown fury of a mother protecting her young.

With her face flushed with color and those green eyes blazing at him, she looked more beautiful than he'd ever seen her. To his dismal surprise, he found himself wanting her again, this time more fiercely than he had a right to.

Fighting to suppress his own instincts, he kept his voice low to keep it from breaking, praying she would hear only the truth behind his words and not the fear that shook him to his core.

"You have to admit there's a resemblance."

Tersely, she replied, "If I thought that every dark-haired, dark-eyed man on the street could be Jason's father, I'd spend the rest of my life looking over my shoulder."

"Those traits you spoke about before, I recognize some of them. I was just like him when I was his age."

"So was I. It's called being a kid."

"All right," he said, his frustration mounting, "you're determined to think this thing is just a coincidence. But what if it's not?"

She stood in front of the kitchen counter, her arms folded across her chest, a look of pure distrust on her face. "You haven't offered me any proof that it isn't."

"I don't have that kind of proof," he said. The slight relaxation of her features would have been imperceptible had he not been watching her so closely. He weighed his next words carefully, knowing their importance. "But you do."

Dory was watching Ben just as intently, searching for a sign that this was all just a sick joke. "Proof?" she tossed back at him. "What proof do I have that would prove Jason is your son?"

"How about a birth certificate?"

"What makes you think I have one?"

"Don't the adoptive parents get the birth certificate? What about those kids you hear about who go rifling through their parents' dresser drawers and come across birth certificates and discover they've been adopted?"

To Dory, it was a pathetic attempt to reclaim something he had lost. If she weren't so angry, she might have felt almost sorry for him. "I've never known it to happen, but I suppose it could. It all depends on what the birth mother wants. In my case, she demanded total anonymity. The records are sealed. I have all the vital statistics, time of birth, weight, inches, but not in the form of a birth certificate." Stoically, she added, "Sorry."

"There's another way to find out if I'm his father," said Ben, undeterred. "DNA testing."

"That's out of the question! Jason had his tonsils

out last year and he had nightmares for weeks over the blood test. I'm not about to put him through that kind of thing."

Ben put his hand up to staunch her reaction. "No, no, I wouldn't want you to. Of course not."

"Besides, in order for it to be even remotely possible, we would have to have used the same attorney, and what are the chances of that happening?"

In the face of the odds she was stacking against him, Ben felt his hope slowly slipping away. "My son's adoption was handled by an attorney in Manhattan by the name of Celina Bonham."

There was a soft intake of breath. Dory's voice emerged scratchy and raw. "Celina Bonham is one of the best family law attorneys in the state of New York who specializes in private adoptions. It's not so inconceivable that we would have used the same attorney."

"But you just implied the odds were too great for that to happen."

"They are. At least I think they are."

The truth was, Dory didn't know what to think. Every word of Ben's shocking pronouncement was a blow to her heart. That he could be Jason's father was unthinkable.

Was it merely coincidence that he'd come knocking on her door that first morning, or had he seen Jason in town and followed him here? What if it was just a crazy coincidence after all? But what if it wasn't? What if it was his intention to try to take Jason away from her? With all the unanswered questions swirling in Dory's mind, only one thing was certain. Someone's heart was bound to be broken.

Chapter 6

A breeze full of springtime and dogwoods wafted through the carousel. The high sun was caught in the gilded panels as Dory applied a coat of white primer to one of the horses.

When that was dry, she would use the same artist's oils that were used in paintings to add subtleties, and shade and soften for expression. As with an oil painting, by the time she was finished, she would have used a dozen layers of color to give the right richness and underglow to a rippling flank or a flowing mane.

Working with the horses was like a tonic to her. Often, when she was feeling lonely and regretful, she would seek them out, finding consolation in their stoic company.

They were her oldest and truest friends, her link to happier times, to memories of growing up surrounded by her parents' love.

Losing her parents had been the first blow to her

heart, leaving it as fragile as glass for the disappointments that would follow. She didn't think there was anything that could hurt her more than losing them, except perhaps losing the Dutch Mill, or Martin...or Jason.

That last thought brought with it a pain that was almost unbearable and which not even her gilded-hooved friends could assuage. A pain that was worsened by the nagging little voice at the back of her mind that kept repeating, "Can it be? Can it be?"

The worst part of it was that her feelings for Ben had begun to grow stronger. First there was his kiss, tender, tentative, saying more than mere words could ever express with its lingering softness over her lips. In the days that followed she had actually found herself looking forward to seeing him at breakfast.

In the past, breakfast had always been such a haphazard affair, with Martin routinely up at the crack of dawn, Jason refusing everything except cereal, and Eddie sleeping one off until noon, that she had forgotten how wonderful something as simple as making breakfast for a man could be.

When had it begun, this slow and steady shift of emotion within her? When had the handsome dark-eyed drifter pierced the hard shell of her resolve and pricked the tender core deep inside? Like the wind, he had slipped in without notice, stirring up her emotions and creating havoc in her mind.

She should have trusted her instincts that told her not to hire him in the first place. There had been something about him from the start that put her on edge. She told herself it was the way he stared at her with those dark, probing eyes, and the fact that she knew so little about him. She didn't want to admit that maybe it was her attraction to him, slamming into her with the force of a locomotive, that made her uncomfortable.

It was her feelings for Ben that angered Dory the most. She could fight in court his attempt to take Jason away from her, but how could she fight these feelings that sprang from somewhere deep within and which would not be denied?

Over and over again she asked herself how she could have been so wrong a second time. First Eddie, and now a man who could hurt her even worse.

Torn between her budding feelings for Ben and her desire to protect and keep her son, Dory tried to concentrate on her work, but she could not. In her heart she knew she had to find out if what Ben suspected was true. Certainly not for Ben's sake; she'd be damned if she would help him. But for Jason's, knowing that she could not deprive her son of the right to know his father, and for her own, knowing that she would never forgive herself if she did not somehow find the courage to do the right thing.

She heard the car and knew that Martin had returned home, with or without the paint she didn't know, since she was doing her best to avoid Ben and had no intention of going over there to find out. Lunchtime came and she let the two of them fend for themselves. She could just picture the scene in the kitchen, Ben with his hideous secret threatening to ruin their lives, Martin unsuspecting, as they sat at the table eating tuna-fish sandwiches. But as the hours passed, she knew she couldn't avoid Ben forever. She knew also that she really had no choice. She had to help him.

It was well past noon when Dory stepped off the carousel and went to the house. She came out a few minutes later, looking pale and feeling apprehensive. Drawing in a supportive breath, she went to find Ben.

The first thing she saw when she rounded the corner of the shed was the games of chance. Some still wore their coats of old, peeling paint. Others were painted in bright new colors that shone in the sunlight, with big bold lightning streaks, exclamation marks and spirals in colors that contrasted wildly with the backgrounds.

Ben had been right. Day-Glo was the way to go. The transition was amazing and exciting, and as she stood there admiring his work, Dory could just imagine all the eager kids lining up to try their luck on opening day.

A glance around revealed no sign of Ben, and the courage she had talked herself into began to dissipate. Maybe tonight, when Jason was asleep in bed and Martin was snoring softly in his rocking chair on the porch, maybe then she would confront Ben with all the questions running rampant through her mind, like what would he do if they found out that Jason was not his son, and what would he do if they found out that he was?

She was on her way back to the carousel when she saw him. He was sitting on the ground, his back pressed against a tree, knees pulled up, his head in his hands. For a moment she thought he was weeping, and for the first time she was acutely aware of just how much this was affecting him.

Upon closer scrutiny, however, she noticed that his body was perfectly still, and no sound came from him. Good. She didn't want to feel sorry for him. Yet even as she approached, she felt a subtle tugging on her heartstrings.

The sudden tension in the air told Ben he was not alone. His head came up from deep thought to the sight of her.

Even now, looking unfriendly and immovable, she was beautiful. Sunlight sparkled like copper pennies all through her hair. In the bright light of day her eyes shone as green as emeralds. Her cheeks were tinted, no doubt from the anger she had every right to feel.

He couldn't blame her for hating him. Just when he'd begun to feel as if he were making some progress in gaining her friendship, he himself had driven this terrible wedge between them.

He'd been sitting there, agonizing over how on earth he was going to bridge the gap and, more important, tell her the rest of it, about Allison and prison, without destroying whatever chance he had of convincing her to help him. More than anything now, he needed her understanding, the one thing he wasn't likely to receive.

He got up from the ground and dusted himself off. Somewhere in the tangle of his emotions he found his voice.

"Did you see the games?"

She answered grudgingly, "Yes. I've got to admit you were right."

"I'm glad you like them." He shifted awkwardly from foot to foot, feeling uncomfortable with their small talk when there were more compelling issues at hand.

"Ben, I—"

"Dory, I—"

Their words shot out in unison and ceased just as abruptly as each turned away in a fluster.

His next words emerged unsteady and unsure. "Were you going to say something?"

"You first," she urged.

Ben licked his lips nervously. In his mind were dozens of things he could have said to her, but to his own surprise, it was his heart that spoke.

Unconscious of the physical gesture, he reached his hand out to her, palm up, empty and pleading, and said, "Dory, you've got to believe that I never meant to hurt you. I had no idea when I showed up here that something like this would happen."

She looked down at the outstretched masculine hand, its strong brown fingers slightly bent and beckoning to her. She closed her eyes in anguish at the appeal she heard in his voice.

"I don't know what to believe anymore."

He came to stand behind her, only inches away but not daring to touch her. "Believe that I would never do anything to willingly hurt you."

"Is that the operative word, Ben? Willingly?" She turned to face him. "I see. You wouldn't willingly hurt me, but if I get in the way, so be it." He was standing so close that she could feel his heated breath rustling the hair along the side of her face. "Well, I can tell you this. If you try to take Jason away from me, I certainly *will* get in the way. I'll fight you all the way to the Supreme Court if I have to."

"What makes you think I want to take him away from you?"

Dory's eyes narrowed, suspicious of him, like slits of green glass. "You don't want him?"

"Of course I want him, but, who knows, maybe there's another way. Earlier you mentioned visitation rights. Maybe we could work something out."

Uncertain whether or not to believe the sincerity she heard in his tone, and needing to know more about the man to whom she might have to give up her child, Dory questioned bitterly, "What would make a man give up a child in the first place?"

Ben swallowed hard and answered, "I didn't know about him. My wife and I were separated at the time. I didn't even know she was pregnant."

"You had time to come forward before the adoption was final. Why didn't you?"

It was the one question he dreaded most to answer. His muscles tensed beneath his denim shirt. Carefully, he replied, "I was out of her life and didn't know I had a son until he was three years old."

"It sounds like you didn't know a lot of things."

His look turned stony at the disparaging tone. "I didn't. But I do now."

She arched a slim brow at him. "Oh? And just what do you know now?"

"I know that I may have found him."

"Based on what? A hunch? A feeling? Because Jason has dark hair and eyes? Because the same attorney happened to have handled both adoptions?"

"Yes, to your first three questions. And as to the last, because maybe it was the same attorney who handled *one* adoption."

"Do you know anything about your son, anything at all that would convince me that you're right?"

"Only that he's living somewhere up here and that he's the same age as Jason."

Dory was exasperated and angry and frightened all at the same time, and now she was flabbergasted. "That's it? That's all you know, and based on that you want to put my family through a nightmare?"

"There are too many coincidences," he argued. "And a feeling. Here." He brought a closed fist down hard over his chest. "Don't tell me you never had a feeling about something that wouldn't go away and that turned out to be right. If we can't depend on our instincts, what can we depend on?"

"You're right about that. And my instinct is to protect my child."

He bit back his abject disappointment. "Of course, I understand. I can expect no help from you."

"That's not what I said."

In answer to the questioning look in his eyes, Dory spoke her next words carefully, not wanting to arouse in him any unwarranted hope. "What I mean is, while my instinct is to protect my son, it is also not my intention to stand in the way of him knowing his father. We'll never know if that's you unless we find out. That's why I phoned the attorney before I came out here to speak to you. We have an appointment to meet with her on Friday at noon. We can drive into town and take the train into the city."

"Dory, I—I don't know what to say, except thank you."

"Don't thank me, Ben. Like you said that first day, I'm not doing this for you. I'm doing this for me and Jason and Martin. And speaking of my grandfather, I'd rather you didn't mention this to him. I'll just tell him that we have to go to pick up supplies. There's no sense in worrying him over something that isn't likely to happen."

Her voice was no longer hard-edged, but soft, with that vulnerable little scratch that brought Ben's protective instincts to the surface. But if he had learned anything about her today, it was that behind the delicate facade, the sad, green eyes and softly aching voice, beat the heart of a survivor.

He was shocked by what she had done, until he remembered that streak of fairness that ran through her like a river, deep and sure, and he knew that she could not go against her nature.

Wishing that he felt an iota of the confidence she must be feeling, he said, "You're that sure of yourself?"

"The word is hope, Ben. Isn't that the one thing that was left inside the box?"

Chapter 7

Ben looked out the window of the taxi as it weaved and dodged its way across town. The streets of Manhattan were thick with congestion. Everywhere he looked people streamed out of the buildings and subway exits, all converging to form one colorful moving mass of humanity. It was all just the way he remembered it. The energy, strung like a network of live wires all up and down the streets and avenues. The bustling pace of people always in a hurry to get somewhere. The throbbing rhythm of honking horns and sirens.

He used to be a part of all this, once, in what seemed now like an eternity ago. He used to love this place. The energy and the madness of it had helped to fuel his own creativity. A part of him resonated with that energy even now.

Yet as the taxi jockeyed for position through the crowded streets, another part of him felt strangely disconnected from it all. The city was too big, too fast, and filled with too many bad memories.

Ever since Dory had announced that she'd made the appointment with the attorney, he'd been apprehensive over whether the woman would remember him. It couldn't have been every day that a man fresh out of prison showed up at her office looking for his son. With the exception of a few more hard lines etched around his eyes, he reasoned that he hadn't changed much externally in three years. She was bound to remember him once she heard his name. He paled at the thought of what he would do if the subject of prison came up. It wasn't the way he wanted Dory to find out.

It wasn't that he didn't want Dory to know. On the contrary, his need to open up to her was stronger than ever, particularly in light of the bomb he had dropped in her lap about Jason. He had to be honest with her. He wanted no lies between them, not if there was the possibility that they might share a little boy's life.

He turned from the window to look at Dory seated beside him on the ripped vinyl seat. She was wearing a white dress with tiny red polka dots spread across the fitted bodice and flared skirt. A matching fabric belt was cinched about her waist. His eyes were drawn to her legs. The heels on her red leather shoes were just high enough to give her calves a flattering curve and her ankles that sexy little turn that made his eyes linger.

It wouldn't have surprised him to find out that she had bought the dress at a thrift shop or vintage clothing store. He suspected that her penchant for auctions and antique shops was due only in part to her search for carousel horses, but mostly because of her genuine interest in remnants of the past. She was an alluring combination of old-fashioned sensibilities and modern realities. She was a woman whose tastes and mannerisms reflected a gentler era, yet she got by on intelligence and twentieth-century independence. She was simple and complicated at the same time, one trait luring him like a candle in the window, the other propelling him right through the glass.

Her slender hand was resting on the black vinyl seat between them. He resisted the urge to envelope her fingers in his, to tell her with his soft cradling touch that everything would be all right, when he knew that it wouldn't be, not once she heard about his past. He was seized again by the fear that she would find out from the attorney. The words scratched painfully at the back of his throat when he opened his mouth to speak.

"Dory, there's something I have to—"

His effort to explain was aborted by the sudden lurch of their bodies when the taxi screeched to a halt at the curb.

"This is it," the driver announced.

Ben's words retreated back into silence as he reached into his pocket for the money to pay the fare. He caught up with Dory on the sidewalk, and they entered the building together.

She had been reticent for much of the morning. Now, as they stood before the elevator door, she broke her silence to ask, "You were about to say something?"

The elevator doors pulled back and half a dozen people emerged into the hallway. Another half-dozen crunched forward into the elevator, bringing Ben and Dory along with them.

The silence inside the elevator was deafening. All eyes were averted as they ascended. Ben felt doomed. There was nothing left for him to do now except pray that the attorney did not bring up his past and destroy his chance for the future.

For Dory, who had grown up in a small upstate town, New York City had always held a chilling allure. Its bigness never failed to awe her. Yet as vibrant and thrilling a place as it was to visit, it had always felt good to be home again. As she sat on the couch in the reception area, her hands resting in her lap, her eyes averted to the carpet, whatever awe she once felt was replaced by the fear this particular visit inspired. With Ben's taut presence beside her, she knew that the only thing here for one of them was heartbreak.

The minutes ticked by with agonizing slowness. The air was thick with tension. Dory was remembering the last time she had been there, sitting on that very couch. She had been so utterly happy then with the adoption of a baby boy. Would the results of her visit today reverse all that and bring her world crashing down around her? Was it to be Ben's happiness at the expense of her own?

It seemed to take forever until they were shown into the attorney's wood-panelled office. An imposing figure in a tailored dress and tortoiseshell glasses rose to greet them.

Dory introduced herself and Ben, then said, "It was good of you to see me on such short notice. I don't know if you remember, but you arranged an adoption for me and my husband some years ago."

Celina Bonham extended her hand to both of them and motioned for them to be seated. "Of course, I remember you, Mrs. McBride. I never forget a client.

When you phoned the other day, you said the matter was urgent. What can I do for you?"

Dory cleared her throat and began nervously, "You can help me find out the name of my son's biological father."

The woman gazed at her forthrightly. "That's an odd request. May I ask why you want that information?"

Despite shaking like a leaf inside, Dory's voice remained level. "I have reason to think…that is, it's possible that my son's biological father may be someone I know. If that's the case, I would naturally want him to be a part of my son's life."

"I see. And have you discussed this with the man you think might be your son's biological father?"

"Yes, I have. In fact, it was he who approached me about it."

In a worried tone, the attorney questioned, "How is that possible? I went through your case file this morning to refresh my memory of it. It clearly stated that all parties were to remain strictly anonymous."

Dory shifted uncomfortably in her seat. "It's a long story. The thing is, we think…that is, Mr. Stone thinks he might be my son's biological father. We would like to know for sure."

The attorney leveled a look at Ben from over the rim of her glasses. "Is there a reason why you think that, Mr. Stone?"

To the cross-examining tone Ben replied, "You handled an adoption for my wife at around the same time that you handled the adoption for the McBrides."

"You say your name is Stone?"

Ben knew that she was reaching back into her memory for the facts surrounding the case.

"Yes, of course. A rather unusual case, as I recall. The father didn't come forward for, what was it, three years?" She took a long, hard look at him, as if to satisfy herself that this was the same man who had appeared before her back then. "I remember telling you at the time that I could give you no information on the child's whereabouts. Those records were sealed and remain so."

"I'm not asking for those records to be unsealed."

Her look turned mildly suspicious. "Tell me, Mr. Stone, how was it you found your way to Mrs. McBride?"

He wanted to tell her to stop calling Dory Mrs. McBride, because, on top of everything else that was going on, there was that unexpected pang of jealousy that came every time he thought that she had been someone else's wife.

He answered tautly, "Coincidence."

"How interesting. Now, let me see if I understand the situation. You wish to know if you are the biological father of Mrs. McBride's child?"

He wanted to shout at her, "Yes, yes," and ask why was she making it so difficult. Telling himself that she was only doing her job and that she had every right to question him, he forced a calmness into his tone that he did not feel, and said, "That's exactly right. And Mrs. McBride has consented to that knowledge being made available to me. To us." They were in it together, after all, weren't they?

The attorney sat back in her leather chair and folded her hands before her. Lifting one finger into the air, she said, "Ah, yes, but will the court consent to that knowledge being made available?"

"The court?" Dory questioned. She glanced at Ben,

to see if he was as surprised as she was, and saw the keen disappointment that flashed through his eyes. Even now, at a time like this, she felt for him.

"Those records are sealed," said the attorney. "We would have to petition the court to—"

"Do it."

Both women turned in unison to the sound of Ben's voice that issued harshly from his throat.

"Mr. Stone," the attorney objected, "we cannot simply petition the court to unseal the records based on coincidence. You must understand."

"What I understand is that five years ago my son was taken from me without my consent or my knowledge."

"How do you know your child was a boy? Perhaps it was—"

"Because I know." He would not betray the law clerk's unwitting error, but neither would he let this woman throw roadblocks in his way.

It could have been the dangerous tone of his voice, or the unsmiling features, or the way those obsidian eyes blazed into hers, all daring her to refute him, that made the attorney cease her line of questioning and take a gentler tone.

"You understand, of course, Mr. Stone, that I could not file a petition with the court without Mrs. McBride's consent."

Ben looked at Dory. This was her chance to back out. All she had to do was say no. Her face betrayed none of her thoughts. There was only the familiar expression of sadness clouding her beautiful eyes. Only this time, it pained him to know that he was the cause of it.

Feeling the weight of Ben's stare upon her, Dory

lifted her gaze to his. In his dark eyes she saw his hope and his fear, with one of those emotions so close to being realized.

With her gaze unwavering from his, she addressed the attorney. "I would like you to do whatever is necessary to find out if Ben...if Mr. Stone...is Jason's biological father."

The words were out. There was no going back for either of them.

"Very well, then, I'll have my secretary draw up the petition. When it's ready, I'll send it overnight to you for your signature."

Dory turned away from the silent look of gratitude she saw in Ben's eyes to ask, "How long will it take?"

"It usually takes several months, but I'll see what I can do to hurry this one along. The judge over in family court is a friend of mine. I can probably get it down to a few weeks."

A few weeks, Dory repeated numbly to herself. Would they find out before Memorial Day or after? Would Ben have to stay on after Memorial Day until they learned the decision of the court? And then what? Her mind screamed with questions as she rose from her seat.

"Thank you, Mrs. Bonham. You've been a great help to us."

"You understand," said the attorney, "that if the petition is approved and the records are unsealed, the only information you will receive is whether or not Mr. Stone is the biological father."

"You mean a yes or a no, as simple as that," said Ben.

"That's correct. And if the answer is no, I would

not think of petitioning the court to unseal the records
of your child's adoption, Mr. Stone. I doubt the court
would look favorably on such a request, given the, er,
circumstances of the case.''

Outside in the bright sunshine people rushed by, and
the air was thick with the fumes spewed out by week-
day traffic.

Feeling relieved that, for whatever reason, the attorney had chosen not to bring up his past, he said to
Dory, ''C'mon, I'll buy you some lunch.''

''I don't have much of an appetite,'' she said, ''but
I could use a place to sit down for a while.''

''There's a little French restaurant on the next
block,'' he offered.

She looked at him, eyes questioning out of a pallid
face.

''I used to live not too far from here.'' he explained.

''Oh,'' she said weakly. ''I didn't know that.''

There were a lot of things she didn't know about
him, Ben thought. How and when to tell her everything was foremost on Ben's mind. Yet both of them
had been through an emotional wringer today, and he
sensed that this was neither the time nor the place for
another confession.

Yet somehow he couldn't leave things the way they
were. In an attempt to put things in perspective, he
said, ''It looks like we're in this thing together.
Whether we like it or not, we need each other.''

Having been thinking the same thing, and seeing no
other way around it, Dory replied, ''You're right.
We'll have to put our differences aside temporarily to
work together.''

As they walked together down the block, each felt
hopelessly drawn to the other, for they were reluctant

partners in the painful experience, sharing the same apprehension and fear. And in the shared experience each found a little bit of strength.

Chapter 8

The countryside they drove through was restful and rolling, dotted with small farms whose silver-capped silos glinted warmly in the sun. The streams and lakes were plump with bass and walleye. The towns and hamlets were picturesque with their original seventeenth- and eighteenth-century stone buildings lovingly preserved.

Color was everywhere, from the white and pink shimmering dogwoods, the yellow field grass, the red of newly plowed fields, the green of the apple orchards.

The tension that had accompanied them since leaving the house slowly dissipated. A warm spring breeze wafted through the open windows of the car, carrying with it the fragrance of wildflowers growing unchecked beyond old post and rail fences, and a faint deceptive promise that everything might be all right after all.

With the wind rustling his dark hair, it was easy, almost, for Ben to forget the tense hour they had spent yesterday in the attorney's office. It was impossible to look out at the crystal blue sky dusted with mare's tails, unobstructed by tall buildings, seeming to go on forever, or to gaze upon the fields of primroses and hollyhocks, swells of color in the gently rolling earth, and not feel the tranquility it evoked in spite of everything.

A glance at Dory behind the wheel showed no sign of the worried brow and frightened eyes of yesterday. Her face was smooth and untroubled. There even appeared to be the barest upturn at the corners of her lips. Taking it as a sign that she, too, was affected by the beauty and serenity of the countryside, Ben broke the silence between them to remark, "It sure is beautiful here."

There was no mistaking the ring of affection in her voice when she said, "This used to be all wilderness. James Fenimore Cooper once wrote that from here one could see all creation."

"Is Devil's Corner as beautiful as this?"

"In its own way, it is."

"What do you mean?"

"You'll see," was all she said.

They drove down narrow country roads that were shaded by giant oak trees, now and then making small talk about the beauty and local history of the place, each reluctant to break the spell of the beautiful day by venturing into deeper waters. By silent, mutual consent they didn't speak about their trip to the attorney's office, or the kiss by the carousel, one filled with so much dread, the other with so much passion.

It was a little past noon when they arrived at Roxbury, on the northern slope of the Catskills.

At Bill's General Store, they settled in at one of the small, Formica-topped tables. Although still unaccustomed to the slower pace adopted by everyone around him, Ben sat back in his chair, stretched his lean legs out before him, and waited patiently for the waitress to bring the menus. Looking around, he watched as one by one the regulars, in overalls and flannel shirts, drifted in for lunch, claiming their counter stools and trading gossip. Conversation came slow and lazy, like the dust motes that drifted before the windows.

"What do you think of this weather we're having?"

"Goin' to the town meeting on Tuesday?"

"Saw Jane Mayberry the other day. Waved to her, but she didn't see me. Hate to think I wasted a perfectly good wave on her."

When the waitress brought the menus, Ben opened his and pretended to study it as he continued to listen in on the conversation at the counter.

He found the atmosphere of the small general store that sold everything from lunch to luggage as easy and comfortable as a pair of old shoes. "This is incredible," he remarked. "Everyone's so friendly."

Dory looked up from her menu. "You sound surprised."

He smiled sheepishly, like a kid caught with his hand in the cookie jar. "I guess I am. It's just that there's a simple courtesy here that was missing all the years I lived in the city." Not to mention the time he'd spent in prison, he privately added.

"There's a courtesy that goes even deeper," said Dory. "It's compassion. When my parents were killed, the farmers got together to help out. Their wives cooked food and brought it over. The Holstein Club collected money so we could hire a man to help until we could get on our feet. A few weeks later, when one of the farmer's barns burned down, everyone got together and put up a new one in just a few days.''

"It must have been rough for you, losing both of your parents at the same time.''

She wasn't surprised that he knew about the accident that had claimed her parents' lives. She was aware of the fondness that was growing between Ben and Martin and knew that her grandfather had told him about it. She didn't mind. It wasn't as if Martin had betrayed a secret. He had every right to talk about it if he wanted to. After all, losing a son and a daughter-in-law, the loss was as much his as it was hers.

"I was twelve at the time, old enough to understand what had happened. It was as if a light went out and everything became very dark. Having my grandfather there was an enormous help to me. He's been there through all the hard times.'' She was remembering also Eddie and the difficulty she had in coming to terms with the slew of emotions his death unleashed.

It seemed from the expression that troubled her beautiful face, that her sadness was caused by more than the death of her parents at a young and vulnerable age. It couldn't have been the possibility of sharing Jason with him that affected her like that, he thought as he watched her, because he had witnessed that same sweet sadness in her eyes before he'd ever mentioned his suspicions about Jason.

He recalled both her and Martin's mention of a husband who had died, and he felt an unexpected pang of jealousy at the possibility that she might still be in love with him. And yet, that didn't look like lost love he saw in her desire-inflamed eyes just moments after he'd kissed her. And it didn't taste like love for another man on her lips as she kissed him back.

"What can I get you folks?"

The appearance of the waitress at their table forced Ben's thoughts to take cover.

They ordered grilled hamburgers, french fries and sodas. When their food arrived, Ben took a bite of his and exclaimed, "Hey, this is delicious."

She gave him a wry look and said, "We have managed to keep in touch with the twentieth century, right down to the hamburgers."

He smiled back apologetically. "I guess I had that coming. All I meant was, it's...it's..." He searched for a way to put it all in perspective, and summed it up with a shrug. "It's nice."

The small-town friendliness that impressed Ben was something Dory had always taken for granted. To her, there was no other way to be. Watching him discover it for himself offered a different perspective of the man. He was like a kid on the verge of an awesome discovery, wide-eyed, scarcely able to keep the smile from his face. She had to remind herself that this was no kid sitting across from her. This was a man, in every sense of the word, from the masculine desire that brightened his dark eyes, to the powerful touch of his lips, a man with the capacity to hurt her and thrill her all at once.

When they were finished eating, Dory said, "We'd better get going if we want to get to Devil's Corner and be back home before dark." She motioned for the check from the waitress.

"I'll get that," said Ben.

"No way. I asked you to come along, remember?"

"Yeah, but I don't remember your saying that meals were included." He pulled some singles from his pocket and dropped them onto the table. "We'll go dutch. It's the only reasonable solution."

Wishing there was a reasonable solution to their bigger, more pressing problem, Dory left her share of the check on the table and followed him outside to the car.

Underway once again, Ben settled back in his seat. "The Catskills aren't a bad place to be from," he murmured with appreciation as he watched the scenery pass by the window in streaks of ever-changing color against a carpet of green.

"The natives never refer to themselves as being from the Catskills," she corrected. "Here, hometowns come first. People are from Roxbury, or Roscoe or West Kill or Hurley. The mountains are dividers. There's a lot of people who have never even been to the next town thirty miles away. Everything they value in life can be found right in their own backyards."

For Ben, there was something strangely comforting in the small-town familiarity that she spoke of. Something that had been lacking in his own life for longer than he cared to admit. He couldn't remember when something as simple as a friendly wave had stirred as much warmth and caring in him as he felt right now.

He glanced over at Dory and studied her profile etched against the green panorama outside the driver's side window. She was a product of this environment, a reflection of its quietly stirring beauty. He felt himself moved as much by her surroundings as he was by her. The two, he realized, were inseparable.

A subtle shift in the air brought with it the scent of damp earth. The area they drove through now was cleft with dark, spooky ravines, where solitary bypaths led into the darkness beneath overhung trees, and sign-posts were painted with the diabolical-sounding names of places like Devil's Kitchen and Hell Hole.

Dory drove to a spot that was overgrown with fo-liage and shut off the engine. "Come on," she said, as she opened the door and got out of the car. "There's something I want you to see."

Together they hiked up the clove to the top, where a waterfall spilled a thin ribbon of water down a rocky ledge, over boulders and into the dark shade below.

"It's called Kaaterskill Falls," she said. Her cheeks were reddened by the climb and by the nip in the air that was noticeably cooler. "It's not exactly Niagara, but it's one of the highest in New York."

There were other waterfalls that were more dy-namic, more showy, more overtly beautiful. But there was something darkly thrilling about this place. It was the same kind of thrill Ben derived from standing so close to Dory that he could smell the wildflower scent of her hair. It was the deep, driving need he had to reach out and grab a piece of it for himself, with no reproaches from anyone, least of all from himself.

"I've seen Niagara," he said, "It's volume and not much else."

"They say that Rip van Winkle took his legendary nap not far from here."

Her voice was deceptively calm, sounding as if she didn't have a care in the world. But Ben knew better. He turned to look at her. The ends of her hair blew up in the breeze, one chestnut strand slicing across her face. Absently, she reached up to brush it away. The unhurried motion produced a predictable effect in him. The cotton T-shirt she was wearing was matted to her flesh in places from their hike to the falls, drawing his eyes like magnets.

If she knew how long it had been since he was with a woman, she would have known how crazy it was to have brought him up there. Didn't she know that one step in her direction and all his fantasies about her would become reality? Was she aware of how desperately he wanted her? Did she want him, too? Was that her purpose in leading him to this spot?

Bluntly, he asked, "Why did you bring me here?"

The sunlight was mottled beneath the trees. It was a dark and spooky place, befitting Dory's own dark and fearful thoughts. It seemed an appropriate place to broach an unpleasant subject and shatter the tentative peace they had adopted.

"I want you to know what you'll be taking away from Jason if you take him away from here...from me."

Ben closed his eyes in reaction to the answer he had not expected. Was there no place they could go where that shadow did not follow them? Was there nothing they could talk about that did not worsen the pain of this thing that was pulling them closer together even as it tore them apart?

"This place is as much a part of him as it is of me," she said. "That thing you spoke about earlier, that was missing from your life before, I want that to be a part of Jason's life. I want him to know how special something as simple as a friendly smile can be. I want him to feel in his heart a genuine love for his neighbors and the kind of compassion that saw me through the rough times."

"You think I can't teach him those things?"

"Those things aren't taught," she said. "You grow

up with them all around you and you absorb them into your being like a plant absorbs the sunlight. It becomes as much a part of you as the air you breathe. I don't know anything about you. Where you're from or how you grew up. How do I know you value the same things I'm trying to teach Jason to value? I just can't help but wonder what you're used to if you're so surprised by what you see around you."

In a staccato voice, he explained, "I was an architect for many years. I lived and worked in Manhattan. I made a lot of money. Needless to say, that kind of life is very different from this. But I grew up with a mother and a father. I know what love is, and they taught me some pretty good values."

That explained the precision she had observed when watching him build the plane, and the inherent decency in his nature. Yet it also left a myriad of other things unanswered, like why he had given up a lucrative career for the life of a drifter who performed odd jobs for a few dollars. There were only two things she knew of that could change a man so radically. One was love. The other was sorrow.

"I'm sorry," she said. "I didn't mean to imply that you have no values."

"I don't want anything for Jason that isn't what you want for him."

"That still doesn't tell me what you *do* want."

"Only to be a part of his life if he is my son."

Dory studied him for several moments in the sunlight that slanted through the trees. His dark hair was in need of a trim. Almost brushing the collar of his leather jacket, it was appealing in a careless sort of way. There was not a trace of the five-o'clock shadow that would appear later in the day to lend a rugged quality to his face. For now, it was clean shaven and smooth skinned and unbearably handsome in the softly shifting light from above.

Nevertheless, Dory had to be sure, not just of what he wanted, but of the way he went about achieving it. She couldn't help but wonder about the kiss by the carousel, and whether it been as impulsive as it seemed at the time, or if it had been carefully planned to weaken her resistance and make his entry into their lives that much easier. Her green eyes narrowed upon his face. "Is that all you want?"

And you. I want you. More than I've ever wanted any woman in my life. But the words remained on the tip of his tongue like bitter little pills, and instead he replied, "Of course, that's all. What else would I want?"

A part of Dory felt the sting of disappointment even as she breathed an inward sigh of relief. She lowered her lashes under his hot gaze, and turning away, said, "I think we should go back down."

On the road again, an uneasy silence sat between them like an unwanted hitchhiker. With the serenity of the day shattered by the painful subject, Ben sat with his face turned to the window, deep in thought, while Dory drove with her eyes fixed on the road. A short while later they drove into Devil's Corner.

Dory parked the car in front of a shop on Main Street. A sign in the window read simply Antiques.

"This looks like the place," Ben said dryly. He shot a quick look over at Dory to see her reaction as they entered the shop.

But Dory was oblivious to the mild sarcasm. She wasn't thinking about him at all, in fact. The instant she entered the shop and spotted the carousel horse, she forgot about everything else.

Before her stood two hundred board feet of wood weighing nearly four hundred pounds. Its paint was cracked and peeling. The carved plume on its headstall had been broken off. Both its glass eyes were missing. The color of its flanks was obscured by layers of dirt and grease. The once jewel-studded harness had gaping holes where the stones had been dug out. There were scrapes and nicks and gouges everywhere.

All in all it was the sorriest looking creature Ben had ever seen. Standing beside Dory, he exclaimed, "What a mess."

Dory glanced around and spotted the proprietor talking with a customer by the cash register. Turning back to Ben there was an unmistakable hint of excitement in her tone when she breathed, "It's gorgeous!"

"Are you kidding?"

"It's an old one. My guess is from the turn of the century. That means it had to have been made by one of the master carvers, like Carmel or Muller or Dentzel. Look at that, and that, and that." She pointed in succession to the massive head and arched neck, to the mane and to the body. "They were each carved out of one large block of wood, not with machines or power tools, but a hand-sharpened chisel and a wooden mallet. I'll bet the sanding took forever."

She walked slowly around the horse to inspect it, trying to impart a sense of indifference to the shop owner who glanced over at them every now and then. Inside, her heart was racing.

As she ran her hands lovingly over the scarred withers, she explained in a hushed voice, "There are three poses for carousel horses. Jumpers have all four feet crooked and are attached to the middle poles that go up and down. Prancers have their hooves flashing before them. Standing horses like this big guy are found on the outside row of the carousel. They're usually the most ornate. I'll bet at one time he was a real beauty.''

"Is that what you need? A standing horse for the outside row?''

She smiled at him from across the faded and chipped wooden figure, and whispered, "It's exactly what I need.''

"Can you afford it?''

"If he knows what he's got, no. If he wants to sell what he thinks is just some beat-up old carousel horse, maybe. I'm about to find out.'' She turned to go in search of the proprietor.

"Hey,'' Ben whispered.

When she turned back around, she couldn't help but smile at the thumbs-up sign he gave her, accompanied by a wink for good luck.

From where he stood, it was impossible for Ben to tell by watching Dory if she was making any headway with the shop owner. Even under pressure, she was a study in serenity, her movements graceful, her voice soft. Unless, he knew, it had to do with her child, and then she was as formidable as a grizzly bear protecting her cub. He had to admit he admired her for it.

When she returned, he asked eagerly, "How'd it go?''

"It's more than I want to spend.''

The smile faded from his face. "Gee, Dory, I'm sorry. I wish there was something I could do.''

"There is. Mr. Evers says there's a truck rental place not far from here. You can drive over there with me, and then load this baby into the truck.''

"I thought you couldn't afford it."

"It may be more than I want to spend, and it'll take a good bite out of my savings, but I can afford it."

"Then he doesn't know what he's got here?"

"Oh, he knows."

He understood then what she meant before about the things she wanted to teach Jason. No doubt able to get a good deal more money for the horse, the shop owner had let it go for what was, in essence, a song, to someone who was more in need of it than some wealthy collector.

They left the store feeling lighthearted and giggly, the shadow that seemed to follow them everywhere taking a back seat to the excitement of buying the horse.

At the truck rental place, Dory signed the agreement, tucked it into the pocket of her jeans and went to claim her prize.

They managed to get the wooden horse into the truck where they laid it on its side atop some musty old furniture blankets.

Ben wiped the perspiration from his brow with the back of his hand. "Man, that thing's heavy. I could use a cold beer. How about you?"

Dory hadn't worked as hard as Ben loading the horse into the truck, but the thought of a cold drink was appealing. "I spotted a little grocery store down the block."

They headed off down the street. At the grocery store Ben pulled two cold cans of beer out of the refrigerated case. "It's my treat," he said as he paid the cashier.

She allowed him to pay, feeling secretly pleased by the gesture.

Outside, Ben touched the cold can to his forehead. He could get used to this straightforward, uncomplicated way of life. Where once he'd spent so much time looking down at life through the floor-to-ceiling windows of his office as if he somehow weren't a part of it all, in this place he felt invigorated by the clear blue sky and the warm wet earth. At the Dutch Mill, with Dory and Martin and Jason, he felt a part of something for the first time in a long time.

He glanced over at Dory walking beside him. Her head was tilted back as she took a long cool sip from the can. His eyes lingered on the smooth white column of her throat. His own throat went dry.

She looked so incredibly lovely with her head back and her dark hair spilling to her shoulders. When had the mere sound of her voice become so necessary to him? The scent of her hair as important as the air he breathed? And he realized suddenly, just watching her, that it was more than her son he wanted. More than the pleasure her body could give him. It was, pure and simply, her.

Lost in his longing, he didn't feel the first few drops of rain that fell upon his face.

Dory's eyes flew open at the drops that pattered her cheeks. "Hey, we're getting wet! Come on," she cried as she sprinted off.

The rain shower was quick and sudden, wetting their faces and lifting their spirits even higher, causing them to laugh breathlessly as they scurried for cover beneath a grove of apple trees across the road.

Her husky, impetuous laughter filled him with warmth and brought to mind images of happier times. In those unguarded moments beneath the dripping apple tree, he got his first real glimpse of the person she was underneath the sadness, to the carefree, happy woman she was at this moment. Her laughter was infectious, rousing in him the first real merriment he'd felt since who knew when.

He didn't plan for it to happen. The sudden, unexpected reaching for her, the way his arms wound effortlessly around her, the gentle pulling her closer. But there she was, in his arms, her body softly yielding against his, her damp face upturned, lips parted, waiting for his kiss.

Their mouths met greedily. Dory's body heated up so quickly that the air all around her seemed to catch fire. A small sound that was part protest and part plea issued from her throat. In spite of every inner warning, she moved not away, but closer. Her lips opened, inviting him in, accepting his intrusion. Her fingers slid across his broad shoulders to entwine in the thick black hair at the back of his neck. It was madness to respond to him, but it was a madness that Dory had no wish to be cured of.

How different this kiss was from the other, she thought dazedly. The other had been filled with bitterness and pain and scores of dark emotions she'd been unable to guess at. This one was tender and touching, but no less thrilling.

She was oblivious to everything that had come before this, as if the world had only just begun with this moment. Scores of sensations and feelings overwhelmed her. The savage pounding at her temples, and his swollen arousal pressed against her, threatened to drown her in a whirlpool of passion that went against every better judgment.

For several fierce moments they clung to each other, lips and bodies pressed together in urgency. And then, it was as if a curtain had lifted and the raw light of reality suddenly came on.

Ben was breathing hard when he released her and stepped back. Despite the red-hot heat emanating from him and the hunger still in his eyes, there was a look of guilt on his face. He hadn't meant for this to happen. As it was, things were complicated enough between them. But then he'd seen her eyes, large green orbs filled with excitement, and heard the sound of her laughter, and suddenly he had wanted to possess her for reasons that had nothing to do with Jason, but everything to do with her. Even now, with her cheeks flushed, a look of reproach in her eyes, her lips red and still wet from his kiss, even now he wanted her.

Dory felt drained by Ben's kiss. If his kiss alone had the power to make her unsteady on her feet, what would making love with him do to her? It was something she could not afford to find out. Not entirely sure what had just happened between them, she tried to steady her still-racing pulse by changing the subject.

"I was thinking that maybe you could give me a hand with the carousel."

"I'll hoist him up there for you, don't worry about that," Ben responded, misreading her intention.

"Yes, that. But what I meant was that while I'm working on him, you could help out with some other things. There's a hole in the roof that needs to be repaired. We'll need a final coat of paint and varnish over the floor and the panels can be shined up."

He'd felt close to her just holding her in his arms, but this was different. The simple, straightforward way she asked for his help made him feel closer to her than ever before.

"Sure thing," he said, trying to impart a calm impression while inside he was bursting with satisfaction.

"I thought we could start on it tomorrow."

"But tomorrow's Sunday."

"I know you have Sundays off, but I thought—"

"It's not that. I promised Jason I'd take him fly-fishing on the Beaver Kill."

He wasn't sure he'd done the right thing in promising the boy he'd take him fishing. After all, he was still new at this father thing. He longed to fit into the family picture, but he wasn't certain how to go about it. The funny thing was that despite the unresolved issue between him and Dory, lately he'd begun to feel like the man around the house, while a darker part of him didn't really believe that he could ever have the love and family he longed for.

"I didn't know you fly-fish," said Dory.

"Actually, I don't. Martin's been giving me some pointers. I asked him to come along, so that I don't make a total fool of myself."

He could see the relief that washed over her face, and was stung by the realization that she didn't trust him.

"All right, then," she said, "we can start on Monday, after we return the truck."

Dory wondered at the relief she felt that Martin was going with them. It wasn't that she thought Ben would run off with Jason, although the possibility, no matter how remote, hovered on the periphery of her mind. It was more that she feared encouraging a relationship between them, when there was so much at stake.

Chapter 9

An unrhythmic snapping sound, not quite a hammer, but more than a tap, came from the direction of the carousel.

The first thing Ben noticed as he approached was that the tarpaulins had been taken down. The carousel stood bared to the sunlight in the quiet hours of late morning. Inside, he could see Dory at work with a mallet in one hand, a razor-sharp chisel in the other, tap, tap, tapping on the splintered wood in an effort to make it smooth again.

Her gaze was focused as she worked, unaware of his presence. Her chin was fixed with the purpose of her work, and her hands moved with practiced precision. But it was her smile that gave her away, and it was easy to see with his own eager eyes that she loved what she was doing. He was secretly pleased that she had asked him to take part in something that obviously meant so much to her.

He stood among the maples and the oaks, watching her work in the soft yellow light of the carousel. The sunlight refracted off the gilded panels through a hole in the roof and fell like a shower of copper pennies over Dory's bent head. Could it be that she was finally learning to trust him? Who knew? Maybe she would eventually trust him with the secret to her sadness, or, at the least, trust him enough to hear about his past and to understand.

As Dory lifted her gaze slowly to his, she felt that little catch in her throat, the one that came whenever she saw him. And the jitteriness inside, like a flock of starlings on the wing whenever their eyes met.

She had watched Ben and Martin drive off right after breakfast, Ben at the wheel of the rental truck, Martin following behind in the car, not knowing if she had done the right thing in asking Ben to help her with the carousel. He was bound to ask questions about the fire. Maybe even about Eddie. How could she explain one without the other? And who wanted to unleash those memories? Wasn't it bad enough that she'd been dreaming about them ever since that night? Well, until lately, that is. Lately, she'd been dreaming about Ben.

She turned away lest her thoughts were written on her face, and pretended to focus her full attention on the horse, when all she could think about was the tall, dark-haired man standing on the perimeter of the trees. Caught in the act of staring at her, he appeared not to care, as he came forward with a long, slow stride.

"Back so soon?" she said, her voice level, betraying not a hint of the pandemonium inside.

"The directions you gave me were perfect," said Ben. "And we made no stops along the way."

Martin had wanted to stop in Roxbury on the way

back, but in Ben's eagerness to get back to the Dutch Mill and begin work on the carousel, he had shrewdly commandeered the car in Devil's Corner after dropping off the truck. Now that he was back, he didn't care if Dory asked him to scrub the floor. He'd have done it gladly just for a chance to be with her.

"Do you still need my help?" he asked.

There was the barest hesitation in her voice when she answered, "Sure, come on up."

It had taken all his brawn to lift the heavy horse onto the carousel when they brought it back on Saturday, but the tarpaulins had still been up, and he didn't get much of a look around. It wasn't until he stepped forward and up onto the carousel that he really saw it for the first time.

It was beautiful and it was terrible at the same time. The horses on the opposite side looked in better shape than the ones close at hand. These were blackened by soot, their once colorful raiments bearing the unmistakable scars of fire.

One perfect prancer stood out among the rest. His coat was a glossy russet, his dark eyes polished to a high glow. A cascade of intricately carved and brightly painted roses fell from his ebony mane onto a crimson jeweled martingale. A bridle that looked like it was made out of gold adorned his high, proud head.

Ben whistled softly in admiration.

"Thanks," she said. "I finished him a few days ago. I don't have the time to restore them all like that by opening day, but they'll be presentable enough. That prancer was always one of my favorites, so I spent a little more time on him."

"And what about this one?" he asked of the horse from Devil's Corner.

"I'll do the best I can. He won't be in perfect shape by Memorial Day but, hey, he's almost a hundred years old, he's entitled to a little wear and tear. It adds character."

Ben had no doubt that by this time next year they would all be looking as wild and as beautiful as the prancer. Eager to do what he could to speed the process, he asked, "So, what do you want me to do first?"

Dory traded in the mallet and chisel for a sheet of sandpaper and began to gently smooth out the areas she'd been working on. "You mentioned the other day that you used to be an architect."

His muscles stiffened at the reminder. There was no reason to fear her knowing that about him, he reasoned, unless it led to further questioning about his life during those years. And then he'd be forced to tell her the secret he'd been keeping about his past, the one that was sure to wreck not only whatever chance he had of making Jason a part of his life, but the slender thread that was slowly developing between him and Dory.

Forcing a nonchalance he didn't feel, he replied, "That's right."

"Well, short of building me a new roof, how about repairing the old one?"

Looking up, he saw a jagged circle of blue sky beyond the charred wood. "What happened here?"

Dory answered calmly, "You'll recall I mentioned we'd had a fire."

"Sure, but that roof is practically gutted. It must have been one helluva fire."

She flicked her tongue over lips that were growing suddenly drier. "Can you fix it or not?"

"I can fix it, but it'll take more time than we have to get it looking as good as new."

"How about just patching it up?"

He shrugged. "You want it patched, I'll patch it."

Ben's mind was already at work on devising a better roof, one with a deeper pitch. Copper, maybe, to glisten in the warm spring sunshine. With an intricate network of wooden struts inside that he would pick out himself from the sawmill. When he was finished, the ceiling of the carousel would be as beautiful in its way as the horses Dory was refurbishing. What a treat it would be for the customers who chanced a look upward to find something beautiful. Why not? he thought with a little bit of arrogant pride. She wasn't the only one who was good at what she did.

It was astonishing the way it all came back to him so easily, the planning and the detailing, the balancing of forces and the combination of materials, the eagerness to get to a piece of a paper and a pencil to sketch it all out. The enthusiasm he'd once had for his work was suddenly back. The only difference was that back then it had been for buildings. Now it was for a carousel roof.

Jamming a retractable tape measure into his back pocket, Ben climbed up on a ladder to take the measurements. "Where do you get your timber?" he called down to Dory.

To the steady little scratchings of the sandpaper, she replied, "There's a sawmill outside of Libertyville. You can call them and tell them what you want and they'll deliver it. My credit card is on the desk in the den. You can give them that number."

"Won't they question me about using your card?"

"Word travels fast around here. They know there's

a man working at the Dutch Mill. Besides, my grandfather uses it all the time. How do you think he bought
the paint for the games of chance?'' She shrugged. ''I
guess people are a little more trusting around here.''

Trusting? Or downright crazy? Ben wasn't sure
which as he climbed down with the measurements in
his head. Taken back by the matter-of-fact way she
offered her credit card, and the apparent trust that
came with it, as if it were the most natural thing in
the world for her to do, he announced, ''I'll be right
back,'' and jumped down off the carousel.

Dory watched him jog off in the direction of the
house in long, graceful strides. In her mind he had
already proven himself to be an honest man, to a painful fault, if their dilemma over Jason was any indication of it. It wasn't with arrogance or belligerence or
even overwhelming confidence that he had told her he
thought he was Jason's father. She had seen the tortured doubt in his eyes when he had admitted his own
uncertainty, and in her heart she knew those were not
the reactions of a dishonest man.

''They'll deliver it tomorrow morning,'' he said
when he returned a short time later. ''Meanwhile, this
floor looks like it could use a good refinishing. The
varnish and most of the paint have been singed right
off.''

''I bought a sander and a buffer a few weeks ago
at an auction,'' said Dory as she switched back to the
mallet and chisel. ''They're in the shed. I tried to use
the sander once, but I cut myself, and I've been avoid-
ing it ever since.''

''How'd it happen?'' he asked.

''I was lifting the thing onto the carousel, when my
hand slipped.''

"I meant the fire. How'd it happen?"

She had been talking away, not paying much attention to where the conversation was going as she focused her attention on the horse, when her movements ground to a sudden halt.

She tried to continue, but her hand was trembling. Afraid that she would make a mistake and needlessly nick the wood, she laid the mallet and the chisel down and pretended to examine the horse, while secretly she gathered her thoughts about her.

"When I work out here at night, I bring a kerosene lantern with me. One night, I don't know, I must have knocked it over. The next thing I knew, the carousel was in flames."

Ben's glance around confirmed that only part of it had sustained any real damage. "I'm surprised the whole thing didn't go up, with all this wood."

"It started to rain. That rain was like a miracle. It's what saved the carousel, and in turn, the Dutch Mill." Softly, she added, "That's why I never mind when it rains."

"I got that impression yesterday," he said, smiling. "You seemed to enjoy the rain on your face. Although where that rain shower came from I'll never know. That sky was blue only minutes before."

The rain wasn't the only thing that had come from out of nowhere. So had his kiss, and her shameless response to it, and the flood of emotions it unleashed in her. She turned her inflamed cheeks away from him and, struggling for composure, began to work again.

"Wouldn't it be easier if you used power tools?" he asked, shifting the topic away from the events of yesterday once he saw her flushed face.

Grateful for the change of subject, she replied, "I

only use hand tools. There's a lot of subtle stuff you can do that you just can't do with power tools."

Curls of wood flipped away as she worked the chisel around the arch of the eye socket. "I'll do this side first. It's what we call the romance side, the side that faces the crowd. That way, at least he'll look presentable to the customers on opening day."

"You're very good," he said frankly.

Dory blushed. "Thank you. I majored in art in college, and I've always had a love for this old carousel. I'm lucky that I was able to use one to help the other."

"Did you ever think about doing it for a living? Restoring old horses, I mean."

"Lately I've been thinking that after the carousel is finished, I might try my hand at carving my own horses."

"Is there a market for new horses?"

"They made a comeback about fifteen years ago when collectors discovered the art value of them. People who commission carousel horses are usually looking to put them in their homes as an art piece."

"Would you give up running the Dutch Mill?"

She looked up, her genuine surprise registered on her face, and answered without hesitating, "Of course not. The Dutch Mill is more than my livelihood. It's my life. But we usually close down for the winter months, and I could carve the horses then. Now that we'll be up and running again, maybe I can save enough money to have the barn heated so I can work in there."

He envied her ability to look and plan ahead. Three years in prison had taught him not to look beyond today. But then he had stumbled across this charming place and its inhabitants, and found himself thinking about the future, and imagining what a quiet family life like Dory had might be like.

"It sounds like a good plan," he said wistfully. "I wish there was a way I could make a living out of making model planes."

"How's it going on the plane? Is Jason holding you back?"

"Not at all. He's a pleasure to have around. He seems to really like helping me with it."

She had spoken impulsively, and was sorry for it when she experienced a little stab of jealousy knowing that Jason was having a good time with Ben.

She didn't want to share her son with Ben, or with any man for that matter, unless that man was her husband. Wasn't that the way it was supposed to be? And yet, the man who had been her husband had been incapable of being Jason's father, while this man, who could very well be Jason's father, wasn't likely to ever be her husband.

It wasn't because she didn't have feelings for him because, God help her, in spite of everything, she did. It's just that it had gone so wrong before, she could not bring herself to think that a successful marriage would ever be in her future. And then, of course, there was Ben, whose kisses revealed the same desperate longing she herself was feeling, yet who never said he loved her. She was crazy to think that he might want more than Jason. That he might want her.

It seemed that whenever they spoke about Jason, the fragile friendship that was developing between them in spite of themselves stood in danger of collapse. Yet neither wanted to be the one to cause an irreparable rift between them in the event that what Dory feared, and what Ben hoped for, was true.

Ben didn't think there was any other subject that could fill the air so rampantly with tension, until he inadvertently touched upon another topic when he made an unwitting attempt to change the subject.

"Did your husband help you run the Dutch Mill?"

Dory's extremities turned cold with apprehension. No, she silently begged. No questions about Eddie. She could tell him it was an accident and be done with it, but she knew that his keen eyes would detect a hidden truth, and then what would she do? Admit that where Eddie McBride was concerned, her usually sound judgment had been tragically impaired, and that she carried the pain of it with her each day of her life? Or worse, that because of it she was scared to death to ever get involved again?

"Eddie didn't care much for amusement parks."

Her voice sounded far away and detached to her own ears, but then, it had always been easier for her to deal with the painful memories when she held them at arm's length. The truth was, she'd never really come to terms with them. She just sort of lived her life around them, skirting them as best she could, every now and then bumping into them like they were pieces of furniture out of place.

"What did he do for a living?"

Dory groaned inwardly as the subject deepened. "He tried his hand at a few things," she said noncommittally.

Although Ben sensed her reluctance to talk about her marriage, there burned inside of him a need to know more.

"Do you mind if I ask you how long were you married?"

Dory's throat grew tighter, and it was harder to keep

a level tone when his questions had her bumping into memories all over the place. "Six years. And you?"

"Me?" he echoed, the sudden table-turning catching him by surprise.

"You mentioned an ex-wife."

"Oh, right. It was brief. Only four years." He added sardonically, "Long enough to have the experience irrevocably seared onto my memory."

"Bad divorce?"

"You could say that. Although, it had to have been easier than what you had to deal with."

"Wh-what do you mean?" Her movements stilled.

"I'd rather deal with a messy divorce than with the grief of losing someone I love."

Grief? she thought weakly. Yes, there had been that. And disappointment, and blame, and the guilt of watching Jason grow up without a father. But most of all there was the recurring thought that she had made a dreadful mistake, and unlike Eddie, had lived to regret it.

It was simply too embarrassing to tell him the truth, that while she had grieved for Eddie McBride, she had felt awash with relief at his passing.

"It's not true what they say about time healing all wounds," she said. "The hurt never really goes away. We just learn to live with it."

Ben's voice answered quietly, as if he were thinking out loud as he contemplated his own private hurt. "I know what you mean. Life has a habit of going on after the thrill of living is gone. We all live with bad memories. Some are worse than others. They say that losing a spouse is right up there among the major traumatic experiences of our lives."

When she had begun the day, Dory hadn't expected

an interrogation, no matter how gentle, into Eddie's death. It wasn't in Ben's nature to bully it out of her, yet perhaps if it was, she'd have been better able to deal with it. As it was, his tendency toward kindness made her all but want to tell him. And yet she could not. There were too many unresolved issues in her past. For her to voice them would mean having to come to terms with them. And until she was able to do that, what hope was there in her future for a sound and solid relationship with any man, much less with the handsome, dark-eyed drifter who claimed to be the father of her child?

In a faintly quivering voice, she said, "Divorce must run a close third or fourth, though."

"Don't feel sorry for me," said Ben. "Are you kidding? My life has been easy compared to what you must have gone through." Even prison, that contemptible, hopeless place, with danger lurking in every corner, had to be better than losing someone you love.

Dory edged her way around to the other side of the horse. It was easier to put some distance between her and Ben than it was with the memories his probing evoked.

Tentatively, she inquired, "What makes you say something like that?"

"You didn't say when he died, but from the looks of things around here, I'd say it's been a while since he's been around. Yet you obviously only recently started working on the carousel."

Dory began to grow nervous under Ben's careful observations. With his astute perceptions, what else had he detected? Could he hear her rapidly beating heart? Did he know that inside she was shaking like a frightened fawn with fear that his questions would unearth memories that were better left buried?

"Why, yes, that's true. I began working on the carousel last autumn. But I don't see what that has to do with it."

"Only that maybe you had a hard time getting going again. Maybe you didn't want to do it at all. Maybe at times you still don't."

Dory was aghast at the accuracy of his suppositions. "Well, yes, sometimes that's true. It's been difficult, but not because—"

"You don't have to explain to me," he interrupted. "I've never lost anyone I loved, but then, I've never really loved anyone enough to feel that kind of loss."

"It's not that. It's...it's..." Dory struggled for the words to tell him that she never loved Eddie McBride, that she had never even known what love was until she found herself eager to see Ben's handsome face each morning. Regardless of how badly he could hurt her, against her better judgment, and despite all her admonitions to herself, she was falling in love with him.

"You're right," she said. "I don't have to explain to you. I seem to recall that you have an appointment with a sander and a buffer. You'll find them in the shed."

He didn't mind the abrupt way in which she dropped the subject. He could tell that his probing had upset her, and that was the last thing he wanted to do.

They were both grateful when the noise of the sander made conversation between them impossible without having to yell to be heard above it.

An hour later they broke for lunch, and as they sat at the kitchen table eating, each was content to let

Martin chat away with news of what this neighbor or that was up to. After that, it was back to work, until Jason came home, and then everything changed, the way it usually did whenever any rambunctious child appeared on the scene.

It wasn't until after the polite conversation at the dinner table later that night, and a round of gentle coaxing to get Jason to take his bath, that Dory had some quiet time alone. With Martin outside on the porch smoking his pipe, and Ben and Jason upstairs in Ben's room building the model plane, she was suddenly faced with so much silence.

Within that silence Dory's thoughts swirled round and round. She felt like Dorothy in the tornado, swept up and away on a dangerous wind, only to be plunked down who knew where. In some colorful, faraway dreamland, where Ben loved her for herself, and where Jason had a father and she had a husband? Or in the middle of some land of nightmares, where the past's dark demons were there to haunt her?

Ben's mild probing that afternoon had left her feeling shaken. She had done her best to keep those memories under lock and key. But he, with his dark eyes always hot and intent upon her, allowing her no escape, his voice gently demanding, had brought them all surging to the surface.

Later that night they pursued her into her dreams.

She was in the carousel and it was in motion, the horses moving up and down and swiftly past her as she ran between them. She was breathing hard, and the cold fingers of fear clutched at her chest. Turning over her shoulder, she screamed to see Eddie running after her.

In her frenzy to get away from him, the terror that

gripped her in slumber was as real as it had been that night. The cold grip of his fingers was as painful now as then. As before, the crack of his open palm stung more deeply within than upon the surface of her cheek. In the chaos of the dream she saw all about her the color orange, so bright and terrible that she had to shut her eyes tight against it. There was a crackling sound all around her, and a heat so intense it felt like it was sucking the oxygen right out of her lungs. Somewhere in the distance she thought she heard a baby crying.

Then, in the nonsensical manner of dreams, the scene suddenly shifted, and she saw Jason's smiling, angelic face in close-up. As the picture widened, she could see his hands. Each was held in the hand of an adult as he walked between them.

It was her and Ben, walking with Jason between them. There was something sweet and natural about it, lulling her into a sense of security that proved to be all too false when she looked again at Jason and saw that his face was screwed up in pain and that he was in tears.

With a cry, she realized that she and Ben had begun to pull on Jason's hands in opposite directions, each attempting to pull him away from the other. Back and forth, back and forth they pulled, heedless of his fears in their own bitter purposes. *No! You can't have my son!* she cried in anguish. *But he's mine, too!* came the angry and fiercely emotional reply. And all the while, Jason's voice, crying in the background, "Please don't, Mommy."

Coated in perspiration, Dory awoke with a start. Seeking only to run from the bad dream, she flung the covers aside and jumped out of bed. In her bare feet she fled from her room and the house, mindless of the twigs and pebbles that stung underfoot, and of the cold night breeze that twisted the hem of her sheer white cotton nightgown around her legs, making her stumble and almost fall as she ran.

Chapter 10

The transluscent light of the moon fell in graduated planes through the venetian blinds and across Ben's naked torso as he stood at the window staring out at the night.

Whoever would have guessed only a few short weeks ago the desperate turn his life would take when he stepped off the beaten path and stumbled onto this place hidden amongst the maples and the oaks? If anyone had told him that he would find his son and a ready-made family at the same time, he would have laughed bitterly in their face.

When he had begun his odyssey, he had never even contemplated the reality of being a father. Tonight, as he breathed the springtime air deeply into his lungs, he faced the prospect with hesitation. He'd never been a part of a family before. He didn't know if he was up to it, or if he even knew how.

He shivered, partly with uncertainty, partly at the

feel of the cool Catskill air against his naked flesh. He was about to close the window when he spotted something in the distance.

A pale, ghostly image flitted through the woods. The iridescent moonlight lathered her hair, and the long, lithe outline of her legs was visible beneath the sheer white fabric of her gown. Something tightened predictably inside him. He should have been used to it, but he wasn't.

He figured she was on her way to the carousel. Often, when he was unable to sleep, like tonight, he stood for long silent stretches of time at the window. Several times he'd seen her leave the house and head for the carousel. He would watch, straining his eyes to see against the darkness. Only when he saw the light of the lantern come on and cast a soft orange glow over the surroundings did he feel comfortable enough to get some sleep.

There was something sure and safe in knowing she was out there working on her beloved horses that put his own tortured mind to rest. She was like an anchor, holding him steadfastly in this world when he sometimes felt like he was about to careen out of control.

He watched, and he waited, but no light came on. Something was wrong. He sensed it. He knew it. Turning from the window, he slipped into his jeans and nothing else, and followed her from the house.

He found her standing before the carousel in her nightgown and bare feet. There were tears in her eyes and she was trembling.

A twig snapped under foot, signaling his presence, but she already knew he was there from the scent of him carried on currents of cool night air. She'd know anywhere that unique combination of male musk and the faint, lingering traces of aftershave, creating that sexy, intoxicating ambrosia that was all his own. At any other time her knees would have gone weak at the first hint of it. Tonight, however, it frightened her. His mere presence, in fact, terrified her.

She didn't want him to see her like that, vulnerable, fragile, and all too human beneath the crushing weight of her memories. She had to appear strong and resilient, if not for her sake, then for Jason's.

He was standing behind her, so close that she could feel the heat seeping through his flesh, igniting the air between them. Softly he uttered her name. Her flesh jumped at the touch of his hand on her shoulder as he gently but firmly turned her around.

There was no use trying to hide the tears that brightened her eyes and glistened like dewdrops on her cheeks. Squaring her shoulders, she looked up into his questioning eyes. Through the darkness she could see his concern written all over his face.

His concern was shocking, particularly since it was on his account that she was in this torment. His questions about the fire and her marriage to Eddie had unlocked a door she thought she had closed a long time ago, allowing a wave of painful memories to flood back. She thought she had learned to live her life around them, but suddenly, there they were, all converging to form a solid brick wall around which there was no escape. And it was all his fault.

Feeling belligerent and confused, Dory said, "Don't you ever have the need to be alone?"

Ben dropped his hand to his side, stung by the harshness in her tone. "I'm sorry. I didn't mean to pry. I saw you leave the house, and when I didn't see a light come on, I got worried."

"You needn't worry about me," she said. "I'm perfectly all right."

"Is that why you're crying? Because you're all right?"

Her green eyes flared at him, angry and pleading. "Haven't you done enough? Can't you ever just let anything be?"

"I just wanted you to know that I didn't mean to open up a whole can of worms for you this afternoon."

Oh God, she groaned to herself, he was doing it again. Yet she clung stubbornly to her defenses. "I don't know what you mean."

"Eddie. The fire," he said matter-of-factly. "It seems that whenever one or the other is mentioned, you close up tighter than a clam. You know, Dory, sometimes it's easier to deal with something when you face it head on."

Like the way he was facing the prospect of fatherhood? he thought with self-contempt. That was a laugh, him giving her advice that he wasn't capable of taking himself. Still, it was always easier to solve somebody else's problems than it was to solve one's own, and he of all people knew what it was like to do battle with demons.

"If you ever feel like talking about it—"

Dory laughed nervously. "About what? Really, Ben, you're imagining things."

His hand came up before her face. "Am I imagining this?" With the tip of his finger he wiped away the solitary tear that still glistened on her cheek.

Dory jerked her head away. "What do you expect? You barge uninvited into my life, making outrageous claims, threatening to destroy my family. Did you think I would take all that lightly, Ben? I'm not made out of wood, you know.''

He spoke in a soothing tone, hoping to calm the hysteria he heard growing in her voice. ''No, you're not made out of wood. You're flesh and bone and blood, just like the rest of us. In short, Dory, you're human. It's not this thing about Jason that you're crying over. It's something else. I've seen you when you're defending what's yours. You're a gutsy fighter. But this is different. You're scared, Dory. I'm not made out of wood, either. I've been there enough times myself to recognize it in you, so don't go through the trouble of pretending on my account.''

The first day they met she had felt an uncanny sensation that perhaps he understood what it was like to cling to hope. Yet now, several weeks later, with so much unresolved between them, she resented his ability to see past her lies and half-truths. He was leaving her no place to hide from his questioning. With his gentle probings, and not-so-gentle observations, he was forcing her into a corner. There was no escape, except to give him what he wanted, and that was the truth, no matter how painful it was for her to reveal, nor how terrible it might be for him to hear.

No matter what the outcome was of this thing with Jason, Dory knew that her future would always be haunted by the dark memories if she did not face them. Her voice, when she spoke, scratched painfully at the back of her throat. ''You're right. This is different. This has nothing to do with you.''

She sat down on the edge of the carousel and was silent for many long minutes as she drew in several deep, supportive breaths. She spoke with a hint of resignation in her tone, as if she had somehow known all

along that she would eventually tell him. The words
came haltingly at first.

"Being away at college was exciting, but I was eager to graduate and come back here. For me, this place
is like no other." She gave a little shrug and explained
simply. "It's home. Eddie and I had dated before I
went away, and we wrote to each other. He was from
around here. He was a part of all that was familiar to
me. A part of what I had missed so much when I was
away. I married him soon after I came home."

She paused to reflect on those early days with a
certain fondness, and said with a half smile, "When
you're young and think you're in love, you never
imagine that things can change. But they can." The
smile vanished from her face. "And they did."

Ben sat down beside her. Wrapped up in her torment, Dory hadn't even realized that he wasn't wearing a shirt, until his naked arm touched her naked arm,
igniting a spark within her even now as she struggled
with the words.

"I knew Eddie wasn't really into running the Dutch
Mill, but to his credit, at least he gave it a try. Things
were okay that first year, but Eddie was the restless
sort, always looking for something better around the
next corner. Eventually, he grew bored with the Dutch
Mill. He tried his hand at a few things, but nothing
ever panned out. He used to say that he needed something to take his mind off his problems. We'd been
trying to have a baby without any success, so I suggested that we adopt one. Eddie liked the idea. When
we got Jason, he seemed happy at last. But then things
began to change. Soon he got bored even with that."
She paused, and her voice grew dim with remembering

when she added, "Around that time he started drinking."

Ben wished there was something he could do to banish the pain he heard in Dory's voice and wipe away the tears that began to spill anew from her eyes. But he knew from his own desperate soul-searching that there was nothing to be done. It was like cleansing a wound. The soap and water burned and the iodine stung like crazy, but it was all necessary if there was to be any healing. All he could do was sit there, his arm barely touching hers, letting her know by his presence that she was not alone.

She went in the same softly aching voice.

"His drinking got worse. He lost one job after another because of it." She swallowed hard and said, "He became abusive, not just verbally, but..."

She couldn't bring herself to say it out loud, but she knew when she felt the sudden tensing of his muscles beside her that she didn't have to.

"Why didn't you leave him?" he asked.

"I tried. Twice."

"What happened?"

"The first time I went back when he swore it would never happen again."

She searched his face through the darkness, hoping that he understood and wouldn't judge her too harshly for a wrong decision. "There was Jason to think of," she explained. "I wanted my son to have a father. I wanted to make it work, to believe not just in Eddie's promises, but in my own judgments. I guess I just couldn't admit that I'd made a horrendous mistake. I did marry the man, after all." She gave a sad little laugh, and said, "It's funny how sometimes you think you know someone and you don't know them at all."

"You said you tried to leave him twice. What happened the second time?"

There it was, the connecting thread that led her from one dark memory to another. Pulling in a ragged breath, she steeled herself for the onrush of deepening emotions.

"One night he threatened Martin. It was the last straw. I told him to leave. We had a terrible argument over it. In the midst of it I picked up my lantern and went out to the carousel. Usually, he didn't follow me there. That night he did."

Her hands wrung nervously in her lap and the words rolled from her like snowballs down a mountainside, gathering momentum, hurling her back in time to the terror of that night.

In a panic, she said, "He'd been drinking. He threatened to kill me if I tried to throw him out. All of a sudden his hands were around my throat. I managed to get away from him and started to run, but he caught up with me." Her hand flew to her cheek to soothe the imaginary throb of his vicious slap. "In the struggle the kerosene lantern must have been knocked over. In a matter of seconds the carousel was in flames. Somehow, I made it away in time."

She was unaware of the warm, wet tears that spilled unchecked from her eyes onto her cheeks. Her body shook with sobs as she told him, "The coroner said Eddie was unconscious when he died. He must have slipped and struck his head on one of the mahogany horses."

Understanding, finally, the cause of her deeply rooted sadness made Ben want to protect her even more. Instinctively, he wound his arm around her shoulders. Feeling no resistance, he drew her close to him, giving her the gift of his physical strength to draw on if she wanted it. His voice was a whisper, but it carried his own fierce belief in what he said.

"We all have scars to bear, in one way or another. You never really forget. The trick is learning to live with it."

Dory turned a stricken gaze on him. "You don't understand. When Eddie died, the first thing I felt wasn't grief. That came later. It was relief. How do you learn to live with that?"

Ben tried to maintain his calm while grappling with the impact of her story. "But at least he would never hurt you again. And Martin and Jason were safe."

"Yes, but I can't help but think that if only I had tried harder to be more, I don't know, more..."

"What?" he gently demanded. "Loving? Giving? Hell, Dory, you're just about the most loving and giving person I've ever known. The guy must have been crazy not to see it."

"He didn't deserve to die."

"Nobody killed him, Dory. It was an accident."

"I know that, and I don't feel guilty for his death, really I don't. Nobody could have saved Eddie from the burning carousel."

"Oh, I get it," said Ben. He was just now beginning to realize that there was much more to her secret than she was telling him. "You blame yourself for not being able to make the marriage work. That's it, isn't it? And because of it, you're afraid. You made a mistake once and now you think any other attempt will be a mistake as well."

Dory shrugged out of his embrace and jumped to her feet, unaware of the provocative outline of her legs through the sheer white fabric of her gown, and charged, "How dare you psychoanalyze me."

In spite of her beautiful indignation, her response told him he had struck a tender nerve, and provided the answer to a question he'd been asking himself for weeks. "So, that's why you've tried so hard to keep your distance from me."

"You're threatening to take my son away from me. *That* should be reason enough to keep my distance from you."

"But I didn't tell you about Jason at the beginning, so how do you explain your standoffishness from day one? You've done everything you know to keep me from getting too close to you, and we both know that Jason has nothing to do with it. Tell me something, Dory, are you afraid of getting involved with any man, or just me?"

Her back stiffened with anger at the question, yet she answered candidly, "Don't take it personally."

Ben smiled crookedly up at her. "Right."

"I don't want a man in my life. Any man. I was doing just fine until you came along."

"Sure, Dory," he scoffed, "you were doing just fine. But how about Jason? The kid's crying out for a father figure, so much so that he set his sights on me, of all people. What the hell do I know about being a father? Yet suddenly, there's this kid, reaching out to me, and I'm thinking, 'Man, what's this all about?' If you think that was a can of worms I opened up for you this afternoon, I can tell you that the one you and your son opened up for me is just as powerful."

"Jason, yes, but why me?" she questioned.

"Don't tell me you don't know." Starlight bounced off his dark head that shook slowly from side to side as the truth dawned on him. "You really don't, do you?"

"Know what?"

"How much I want you."

She was stunned by his revelation, and immediately suspicious of it. "But it's Jason you want."

"If he's my son, yes. I don't deny it. But there's another longing inside of me that I've been feeling from the first moment I saw you. I want you, Dory. More than I thought I could want any woman." He lifted his shoulders in a shrug that signaled his helplessness over it.

Her voice was low and unsteady. "Do you think that will sway me?"

He got up and came to stand directly before her. His warm, moist breath whispered against the night, scattering goosebumps across her flesh. "Do you think me that devious?" There was a low undercurrent of anger beneath what sounded like hurt in his voice.

Indirectly, she replied, "I think we do what we have to do to get by."

He gave a contemptuous snort. "Well, at least you didn't call me the devil. Or are you reserving judgment on that?"

He wasn't the devil. He was worse. She had her faith with which to grapple with the devil. But where were her defenses where this mortal man was concerned?

She knew what he meant, and that Jason had nothing to do with it, and it frightened her. To be wanted by him with such fierce candor was one thing, but to want him back with the same intensity was a new and frightening experience.

Want and desire welled up within her, but the need

was the greatest. Never had she felt such overwhelming need as she did just then, standing there in her flimsy nightgown, tears staining her cheeks, inches away from the comfort he offered, if only for tonight.

What would be the harm? she dared to think with some detached part of her mind. To let herself be taken into his embrace, to feel safe in the strength of it, and wanted in the urgency of it. To drown in his kisses and forget, for the time being, the demons that haunted her past and the one that threatened her future.

For one frightening moment desire conflicted sharply with common sense. It would have been easy for her to succumb to the powerful emotions his candor aroused in her. Could she surrender to this man without trading away her son? The stakes were too high, and there was too much for her to lose.

She backed away from him, as if putting distance between them would still her frantically beating heart and bring a semblance of sanity back to her beleaguered mind.

As if reading her thoughts, he said, "Sure, you can walk away if you think it will help. But how do you get away from your own emotions? Your own needs? We try, don't we? We run, but we never quite elude them. Sometimes, they creep up on us at the worst times."

She tried, but how could she hate him for the accuracy of his perceptions, when she sensed that he was speaking as much about himself as he was about her?

"Like now," he went on, his tone low and accusatory. "You want me, too, but you'll be damned if you'll admit it."

Angrily, she complained, "That's awfully presumptuous."

"I'm a presumptuous kind of guy. But I guess you already know that about me."

The carefully veiled reference to Jason made her more uncertain of his motives than ever. "Maybe you're not devious," she conceded. "Maybe what you are is desperate. So desperate for a son, *any* son, that you'll make love to me to try to get *my* son. It's understandable. I would probably do the same thing if I were you."

"You just don't get it, do you?" he charged. "Why is it so hard for you to admit to yourself that someone wants you just for you?"

Her eyes flared wide and her mouth opened, but Ben spoke up quickly to staunch the argument she'd been about to make. "All right, so I can see why you're hesitant. This isn't exactly your standard boy-meets-girl story. Granted, there are some extenuating circumstances. But attraction is attraction. If nothing else, you've got to admit to that."

"I don't know what it is you want me to admit. Am I attracted to you? Yes, in a basic sort of way. Am I stupid enough to do anything about it? Hardly."

"If there's anything you're not, it's stupid. Afraid is more like it."

Dory grew uncomfortable under the weight of his hot, ardent gaze. "You're right. I am afraid. Afraid that you'll take my son away from me."

"Is that the only thing you're afraid of?"

"Of course."

"Prove it."

"What?"

"I said, prove it."

"What do you want me to do?"

"Kiss me."

She looked at him as if he'd gone insane. "What on earth would that prove?"

"That losing Jason isn't the only thing you're afraid of."

"Wh-what else…would I be…"

"Of me. Of getting involved."

"I already told you I don't want to get involved."

"That's right, I remember. You don't need any man. You were doing just fine, in fact, until I came along."

She detested the sound of her own words coming back to haunt her. "Well, yes."

"Then prove it."

"How? By kissing you? Isn't my word good enough?"

"Is mine to you?" he challenged. "When I tell you that I want for Jason only what you would want for him, when I say that it's not my intention to take him away from you, when I put myself on the line by telling you how much I want you for reasons that have nothing to do with him, is my word good enough? Do you believe me?"

"I—I don't know. Sometimes I think I do, and then sometimes I think I don't."

"When I kissed you that first night, when you fell off the carousel. I hope you don't think I planned that, desperate man that I am. But what did my kiss that night tell you? And again, that day we went to get the horse. I didn't plan that one either, although I can't say I wasn't thinking a lot about something like that happening. What did my kiss tell you then? Was I lying to you, Dory? Did you sense that I was conning you?"

She cast her gaze downwards, unable to bear the

scrutiny of those dark, predatory eyes, and answered almost shyly, "No."

"Then don't I at least deserve some proof?"

Dory wet her lips nervously. "Now let me see if I have this straight. I tell you that I don't want to get involved, and you tell me that the only way I can prove it to you is to kiss you."

He answered with a self-satisfied nod.

"And you're counting on reading in my kiss whether what I say is true."

"Actually, I'm not counting on anything. What you say probably is true. If it is, I'll give up."

"You mean you'll leave?" Judging from the way her heart tripped, Dory wasn't sure if that would be a blessing or a curse.

He gave her an apologetic half smile. "Sorry, Dory. I can't do that until I find out about Jason. What I meant was, I'll make him the only thing between us. Nothing more, unless and until you ask for it."

He made it sound so simple, but Dory knew from the pandemonium racing through her blood that there was nothing simple about this man, from his dangerous purpose in their lives to his even more dangerous presence in her soul. His was a deep, dark, complicated existence, its haphazard appearance deceiving. Somehow, when she hadn't been looking, he had slipped beneath her guard to pierce her defenses. Unless and until she asked for it, indeed. His arrogance was infuriating.

She told herself that she could do it, that she could kiss him and still walk away, not unscathed, but at least with that part of her life still in her control. She had made one grave mistake where a man was concerned. She wasn't about to make another one.

Her experience with Eddie had cost her her faith that decent, honest, loving relationships existed not only in her imagination, but in real life as well. But with Ben she stood to lose so much more. She stood to lose her son.

"I won't play these games with you," she said. "I told you I don't want to get involved."

He gave an abrupt laugh. "You already are involved, Dory, whether you like it or not. But don't kiss me if you don't want to. That proves more to me than if you had. But just in case there's any doubt in anyone's mind about what's really going on here, let's get one thing straight."

"Oh? What?"

"This."

His arm shot out to wind automatically around her waist and pull her up tightly against him, lifting her practically off her toes, and crushing the breath right out of her. His body was lean and incredibly strong. There was the same urgency in him that she had sensed that first night by the carousel.

He brought his face to within inches of the outrage he saw stamped on hers. In a softly menacing voice he told her, "Go on, Dory, deny that there's any attraction between us. Deny that what's going on here isn't scaring the daylights out of you. And then, deny this."

She made a small, startled sound that was swiftly silenced by the crush of his mouth against hers. Her body stiffened, and even as she struggled to be released, she knew that resisting was useless, that everything he said was true, and that he was about to prove it.

Chapter 11

Unlike that first urgent kiss beneath the stars, and the tender one under the apple tree, this one was filled with angry emotion. His lips obliterating any protest she might make, he kissed her fiercely, hungrily, over-powering her with the sheer muscular force of his desire.

Dory struggled halfheartedly against the restraint of his strong arms, the bruising pressure of his lips, and the unmistakable press of his arousal against her. But most of all she struggled against the sensations that ignited like tiny fires deep inside of her, spreading white-hot passion through her system like an inferno.

In the midst of the turmoil, he lifted his head and looked at her. In the moonlight that bathed her face he saw that her lips were reddened with the roughness of his kiss. Her eyes were half-closed. Several strands of dark brown hair were matted against the sides of her face. Her cheeks were wet with tears.

"Don't cry, Dory," he whispered. "Nothing can hurt you, not right now, here, in my arms."

Dory's thoughts were swirling like bubbles in a glass of champagne. Ben's breath against her flesh was making her heady with desire. He felt warm and solid against her, his muscular arms wound like protective bands around her.

"You said before you don't want a man in your life. But what about need? Do you *need* a man in your life, Dory? Show me what you need."

The very need he taunted her with sprang up within her, mingling with earthshaking desire. She wanted him, wanted the thrill of letting herself go, of giving herself to him in ways she had only imagined.

Without forethought her palms flattened against his naked chest and began a slow exploration of the smooth, firm flesh, coming to rest upon the two dark circles whose edges were puckered with readiness beneath her fingertips. She could hear his soft intake of breath when she brushed the hardened nipples.

Like skaters on ice, her hands slid smoothly to his arms, fingers flexing around the muscular biceps before gliding upwards, across his broad and powerful shoulders, to clasp behind his neck. The hair that grazed her fingers was like silk, the skin at the back of his neck so incredibly soft.

It was as if she were being manipulated by a will outside of her own. It was her own desperate longing for him that lured her into these dark and dangerous waters, but it was the sound of his voice, a softly pleading rasp at her ear, that pulled her strings and set her in motion.

"Show me," he breathed. "Show me what you need."

She was beyond thinking rationally, beyond saving. Beneath the onslaught of his desire, all she could do was give him what he wanted...what she wanted.

Her fingers obeyed blindly, moving upwards to splay in the thick, dark hair at the back of his head, pulling his face slowly, inexorably closer to her own.

Ben's pulse began to pound, starting at his temples and moving steadily downward, invading every corner of him, throbbing without mercy. His muscles ached from holding his urgency under a tight rein, forcing himself not to rush, when all he could think of was being inside her and having her all around him.

Her kiss was driving him wild, and if it proved anything at all, it was that she was as much a slave to her needs and desires as he was. That she, like him, had kept them under wraps for so long that they surged now to the surface like wild, caged things longing to be free.

He could feel the pressure mounting. He couldn't hold back much longer.

His hands slid over the thin fabric that barely covered her, tracing the outline of every bone in her rib cage. Beneath the cool white cotton her skin was smooth and hot and yielding. He paused at the outer curve of her breasts, thumbs flicking across her nipples, which were hard with anticipation.

Her back arched in reflex at the maddening sensations his teasing thumbs were arousing. She pulled her mouth away, gasping for the breath his kiss robbed her of. Her head fell back, dark hair spilling over his naked arm that held her, her slender white throat bared to him.

He pressed hot, wet kisses to her neck, swirling his

tongue in the hollow of her throat. His whisper was like a breath of hot wind against her flesh.

"Dory," he breathed, "let me help you forget, at least for tonight."

As he held her he could hear the beating of her heart, or was that his own heart pounding savagely through his blood? He was no longer certain of where each of them began and ended. Their lives had become so inextricably woven, just as their bodies were now. In a deep voice that fanned her ear, making her skin jump, he whispered, "Dory. Dory. I want to make love to you. I've wanted it from that first day."

His quick, hot breath against her ear mingled with the thunder in Dory's blood. She opened her eyes to look at him. His face, mere inches from hers, was agonizingly handsome with its desire-hazed obsidian eyes.

He tried to tell himself that having her like this was enough for him, but he knew it wasn't. "There's just one thing," he said, his voice low and guttural against her neck. "You have to want it, too."

There was no escaping the obvious. What a fool she'd been to think that she could kiss him and walk away unscathed. But what if she made love with him? Would she be able to walk away at all? A fan of ebony lashes swooped down to mask her eyes. She turned her face away from his, and her agony mounted as she teetered on the brink of no return.

"Dory?"

She tried to swallow down the lump in her throat that threatened to choke her. Her voice emerged husky and raw with emotion. "You asked me to show you what I need. What else do you need to know?"

"That you *want* me as much as I want you."

No! Dory silently begged. Not that. This was about suppressed desires and the need to fill a sexual ache, nothing more.

Her thoughts were spinning out of control. It was becoming harder to tell the difference between want and need when the thrust of his knee between her thighs sent a spasm of pleasure through her, and when her body felt so open and empty and begging to be filled.

''I want to hear you say it.''

His throaty whisper thrilled her, yet she held back as the last vestige of sanity clung stubbornly within her.

Her hesitation pushed his patience beyond the brink. He'd known her such a short time, and yet it seemed as if he'd been waiting for her forever. All those dark days in prison, and the loveless years preceding them, meant nothing to him at this moment.

He didn't wait for her response. He lowered his head and brought his lips to her breast, drawing the swollen nipple into his mouth through her nightgown, making the sheer fabric wet with his tongue.

She wound her fingers in his thick, dark hair, and with a groan, pulled his head closer against her breast. Want and need converged to form one single passion within her. She wanted him, the triumph of hearing him catch his breath, the weakness that came when she lost her own. She was seized by a sudden, wanton desire to tell him what he wanted to hear, not to satisfy his masculine need to hear it, but to put an end to the terrible pressure of keeping it inside.

Another man might have told her how beautiful she was and how much he wanted her. But this man was not afraid to show it. He used his hot caresses and teasing tongue to tell her how beautiful he thought she was. The breathless voice that sent shivers down her spine told her how much he wanted her. She wasn't surprised by his wanting her, for she'd seen it in his eyes from that very first day. Still, she knew it had taken courage for him to admit it.

She slid her hands to the sides of his face, cupping it, bringing it back up slowly to hers. Putting aside her own fears and doubts, she summoned some courage of her own and said softly, "I want you, Ben. Oh, how I want you."

The words soared through Ben's mind. How many nights had he lain awake in bed imagining her like this, her body all soft and warmly yielding, the breathless words "I want you" spilling from her lips? Yet no matter how many nights he dreamed about it, in this moment of revelation he realized how terribly lacking his dreams of her had been compared to the real thing.

He'd waited years for a feeling like this to come, when all the loose ends would come together, scattering his fears and apprehensions like so much dust in the wind, converging into one conscious, physical act. He had begun to think that only he was that lost, that lonely, yearning for a feeling that never seemed to come. Until tonight, standing amid the horses on the darkened carousel with Dory in his arms, tasting in her kiss a hunger as deep and as desperate as his own.

Whatever doubt still lingered as to whether it was smart to become intimately involved was laid to rest by Dory's breathlessly uttered admission of wanting him, and by the knowledge that she needed him, and that if only for this one night, at least that need was solely for him.

She didn't object when he swept her up into his arms and carried her to a spot between the horses. It wasn't until he had laid her down gently upon the floor of the carousel that Dory realized her feet hadn't touched the ground.

As he covered her body with his, he was torn by two impulses. One was to take her lingeringly, to savor every moment as if it were the first. The other was to possess her all at once, to put an end to the pressure that was building steadily inside of him, threatening to explode in a quick and forceful coupling.

His fingers closed over her soft, pliant breasts, touching and stroking and making her flesh tingle. He lowered his head and kissed their tender undersides, teasing her nipples erect with his tongue before returning his mouth to hers. Grazing her lips with his, he murmured her name over and over again.

She felt the precise moment when the urgency in his touch changed to a gentle, almost shy eagerness, as if he were experiencing this kind of passion for the very first time. Gone was the rough scrape of his calluses against the sheer cotton of her gown. With unhurried tenderness he slid the thin straps off her shoulders and gently pushed it down past her hips, exposing her naked flesh to the ray of moonlight that fell on them through the hole in the roof.

At first he only stared at her, his chest rising and falling rapidly as he drank in the sight of her body as he had imagined it a hundred times, naked and waiting. His face bore the expression of a man who was just now realizing the fulfillment of something he had only dreamed about.

She was so beautiful that it hurt his eyes to look at her. Unable to endure much more of the sweet torture, he lifted himself to his feet. With graceful movements that belied the fierce rush of blood through his veins, he unzipped his jeans and pulled them off.

From where she lay on the hard planks of the carousel floor, Dory blushed at the sight of the male form towering over her. His body was lean and taut, with muscles that were perfectly defined. In the shaft of moonlight from above, his skin looked incredibly smooth and soft. His potent arousal was obvious.

She could feel his manhood graze stiffly against her hip as he dropped to his knees and lay down beside her. His arms moved around her like liquid. With his gentle strength he pulled her over him and positioned her on top of him. He hugged her very close, touching his lips to hers lightly with feather-soft kisses. His hands moved slowly, exploringly downward, following the inward curve of her waist and the soft flare of her hips, coming to rest upon her buttocks, where he cupped the smooth, firm flesh and pulled her tightly against his own swollen flesh.

Her hair spilled down around him, the sexy scent of wildflowers mingling with the smell of the cool, dark earth and the green grass surrounding the carousel. Her breasts were flattened against him, spreading their warmth through him. Her hips were pressed to his, her soft folds gently yielding to his entry.

For one precarious moment in time she remained poised on top of him, the tip of him just shy of deeper fulfillment. He could have entered her with one thrust upwards, but he remained still, every thought and sensation focused on the point of contact and the excruciatingly sweet torment it produced.

He could feel her body straining above him. He seemed to know the precise moment when she was poised on the brink, for his lips sought hers, tongue thrusting deeply into the wet hollow of her mouth. At the same moment her body descended over his as his thrust upward to meet it, coming together in a sweet and savage coupling that went beyond conscious thought or reason.

Dory gasped at the rough, rapid filling. She moved instinctively, matching every thrust, moving atop him in heated motions, creating a friction that drove him wild. It would have been so easy to let himself go right then and there, but this wasn't about just him. She had proven that her need was as great as his own.

With an iron will he used his strength to lift her from him. Ignoring the involuntary little groan of protest that spilled from her throat, he rolled her over onto her back and covered her body with the long, hard length of his. He touched her possessively, his strong fingers kneading her flesh in all its sensitive places, coming to rest upon the soft, dark triangle between her legs. Cupping the tender folds, he probed the wetness within, feeling a sense of triumph in the writhing of her body beneath his.

He kissed her deeply, filling and teasing the wet corners of her mouth the way his fingers filled and teased her.

Dory felt as if she were on fire inside and out. The fingers of one hand caught in his thick dark hair as she pulled his mouth harder against hers and met each thrust of his tongue with her own. Her hand sought his stiff member and closed around it, stroking and kneading and causing a fearsome trembling from deep inside of him.

Mercilessly he explored every inch of her, driving her beyond the brink of sanity, reducing her to the most raw and basic instinct. The tension mounted all about them as she gave back in her eagerness.

Energy and passion raced back and forth between them as they drove each other to heights of pleasure. When he could endure no more of her maddening caresses, Ben grabbed her hand and pulled it away. His breath came in short, gasping bursts as he moved into the space between her legs and slid his member to the place where his fingers had just been.

She was moist and ready and aching to be filled. Her voice was a hoarse whisper, thinning to a trembling plea. "Ben...Ben...now...please."

There was only a deep, guttural sound of reply as he sank fully into her. In compliance, she opened her legs wider, welcoming him into the space, then closing around him and clutching him tightly, feeling his need in each savage thrust, in every desperate kiss, and matching it with her own.

With the stars peering down at them through the hole in the roof, with every nerve screaming for release, Dory's hips rose higher and higher to meet his until at last she felt him arch for a final throbbing thrust, and answered it with a fierce shudder.

They were one writhing, feeling thing, a single flame shooting high into the sky, if not forever, then at least for now. Whatever fears or uncertainties existed before were lost in the tumult as need and want converged in a mass of tangled legs and teasing tongues and in the fulfillment of passion left too long denied.

His skin was damp, the hair at the back of his neck wet and cool against it. He lay atop her, feeling drained. His pulse, which only moments before had been hotter than a rocket on the Fourth of July, gradually eased as the quick, violent flow of blood through his veins began to subside. His weight was upon her, but he couldn't move. Only when he was able to breathe deeply and evenly again, and to think a little more coherently, did he lift himself off her and onto his elbows, slipping out of her velvet warmth.

Looking down into her face, he was caught up in a million emotions. Her eyes were closed. Her cheeks were bathed in the soft rosy glow of their lovemaking. She looked content and fulfilled, like a kitten after a dish of warm milk. And so thoroughly beautiful that he felt the stirrings of renewed desire. He wanted her again, and he knew she would not deny him, yet he made no move to take her again.

He wanted to tell her so many things, like how it had never been for him the way it had been tonight with her, how sorry he was for the unhappiness he had caused her, and how he was falling in love with her. He wanted to tell her all that, and more. He wanted to tell her about those dark years in prison and about the events that preceded them.

Before he could say the words, Dory stirred beneath him, and opening her eyes, asked in a sleepy murmur, "What are you thinking?"

He rolled off her and sat up.

She felt the unmistakable bite of tension in the air. Had she said the wrong thing? Or worse, was he regretting what had just happened between them?

She had been right about him; he was a complicated lover, giving as much as he demanded with a fierceness that both frightened and excited her. He had offered to make her forget, and she had, for the moment, loosing her pent-up passion to a man with the power to heal old wounds and create new ones.

She rose to her feet, bending to scoop up her night-gown, which lay in a soft heap on the carousel floor. With sudden modesty, she quickly slipped it on over her head, shivering at the coolness all about her, when only a short time ago the air had been singed with the heat from their bodies. She was careful, not wanting to say anything that might be misunderstood. They had made love, and for her it had been more intense than anything she had ever experienced. She knew she had broken her own cardinal rule of not getting involved, but somehow, when all she could see and hear and smell and touch and taste was him, it hadn't mattered. Now, however, as she stood there shivering, she was no longer so sure.

In a voice so soft it was scarcely a breath, she said, "There's no need for either of us to regret what just happened. It's not as if it's ever going to happen again."

He could hear the painful question behind her words. He rose and came toward her, his nakedness gleaming in the moonlight.

"I don't regret it," he said. "Not for one minute."

Dory's heart skipped a beat at his uncanny ability to read her thoughts, and to put her at ease.

"And as far as it never happening again, that's up to you. Because if it were up to me…"

He reached for her, encircling her slender waist and drawing her to him.

Their lips met greedily. He was aroused and ready for her again. Without preliminaries, his hands slipped beneath her buttocks, lifting her effortlessly off the ground. Her legs went around him as he slid her down onto himself, locking her body to his in a deep, filling embrace that took them to the brink once more and then spiraled them none too gently back to earth.

She felt light as a feather in his arms as he let her slide slowly back down. "You were saying something about it not happening again?"

The moonlight struck her face in such a way that the shadow of her lashes fell long against her cheeks. He knew that she was blushing beneath them.

"Oh, hell, Dory," he said with a sigh as he thrust one leg back into his jeans. "Neither one of us meant for this to happen, but it did, and I'm not sorry for it. Maybe after tonight it will never happen again, but we're here right now. What happened tonight is about you and me and no one else." He spoke with his back to her, as if he were resigned to it.

She watched him pull his jeans up over his beautiful body, her eyes softly flaring at the way the fabric stretched tightly over his buttocks.

"You can believe that or not," he said. He turned around to face her, pulling up his zipper and concluding, "Still, it doesn't change a thing."

He was right, of course, she thought. The intensity of their lovemaking proved only that each of them was human. Want and need were one thing. But what about love? She noticed that word had never even been mentioned. Maybe it was for the best. Granted, physical intimacy only complicated the issues between them, but she shuddered to think what love would do.

She grasped one of the poles upon which the horse went up and down, and leaned back at arm's length, closing her eyes to the midnight breeze and letting it rustle her hair, which was already tousled from their lovemaking. In a wistful, reminiscing tone she said, "When I was a little girl, I used to think that one day a handsome knight would come riding out of the mist that forms in the foothills and lift me up onto his charger. There's an outcropping just west of here that looks a little like a castle, and that's where I always imagined he would take me.''

She remembered something else she used to imagine. That she would only give herself to a man she loved. She had loved Eddie, briefly. And now here was Ben, to whom she had given herself not just willingly but wantonly. That couldn't have been out of love...or could it?

Dory sighed. ''Sometimes it's fun to still imagine it. How about you? Do you ever daydream?''

Day, night, what difference did it make? he wanted to say. In prison his dreams, whether in sleep or wakefulness, had been the only things keeping him going. ''Sure,'' he said with a laugh. ''I'd love to win the lottery. But then, who wouldn't?''

Dory shrugged, the movement causing one thin strap to slip from her shoulder, creating a predictable tightening in Ben's gut. ''I never really had any money to speak of,'' she said, ''so it never mattered all that much to me. I'm satisfied as long as I can get by and support myself and my son. You must miss the money, though. Didn't you tell me once that you used to make a lot of it?''

With the tip of his finger, Ben gently slid the strap back on her shoulder. ''Come here. I want to show you something.'' He led her to the edge of the carousel. ''See that star up there? That big one that looks like it's winking at us?''

Her gaze followed the direction of his outstretched arm. In the midnight sky one star burned brighter than all the others.

"Yes, I see it."

"How far away do you think it is?"

"In light-years? Who knows?"

"Well, in answer to your question, that time in my life, when I used to make a lot of money, is about as far away from who I am and where I am right now as that star is to earth."

"That far, huh? No wonder you'd like to win the lottery."

"I was just kidding about that. The only things money can buy are possessions and the grief that comes with them. No thanks. I like things much better the way they are now."

"Do you think you'll ever settle down again?" she asked.

"You mean get married?"

"Well, that, or just stay in one place for any length of time."

It was funny, but he didn't used to think so. He went into prison vowing he would never love again and came out even more hardened in his conviction. He'd kept moving from one place to another, never staying long enough to form attachments, not when the hurt of his previous attachment was still so fresh in his heart, and when there was a child somewhere out there that he had to find.

He didn't want to say anything that would disrupt the closeness he felt to her in the wake of their lovemaking. Yet the truth was that he daydreamed often about doing just that, settling down somewhere close by, in fact, in the event their petition was granted and the records were unsealed and it was revealed that he was Jason's father.

"I think about it sometimes," he said.

Even though Jason's name had never been mentioned, Dory was also thinking about him. All this time she'd been agonizing over what would happen if Ben turned out to be Jason's biological father, she had never considered the consequences of what would happen if it turned out he wasn't. For the first time, the very real possibility of him packing his bag and leaving, just walking out of her life as easily as he had walked in, loomed before her.

Suddenly, Dory was frightened, not only of him staying, but of his leaving, and of the impact both would have on her life. She turned away and went to stand beside her favorite prancer. She stroked his arched neck as lovingly as if he were a living, breathing creature. In a soft voice, she said, "For me, there's no knight in shining armor, no castle in the foothills, and no steed except this one."

He heard no self-pity on her voice, only an acceptance of what she felt was her fate. Yet there it was again, that old familiar sadness in her eyes that beckoned him away from the edge of the carousel.

"Say, does this thing work?"

Dory glanced up from her thoughts, embarrassed at having been thinking out loud. "The carousel? Sure it does."

"I haven't been on one of these things in God knows how long. How about a free ride?"

"You mean right now?"

"Why not? Come on, Dory," he gently coaxed her. "What's the harm? Tomorrow we can go back to being responsible adults, but for now..."

She looked down at the hand that waited, palm up, for hers. "Oh, what the heck."

She disappeared between the horses and jumped

down on the inside of the carousel where the gears and movements were hidden behind the gilded panels. Even in the darkness she knew which panel opened to reveal the switches and the lever.

It began with a loud creaking sound as the gears met and set the big machine in motion. Ben felt the floor move beneath his feet and grabbed onto the nearest horse. Dory came up behind him, laughing.

"Does it bring back any memories?"

"You bet it does. When I was a kid my buddies and I used to take the train to Coney Island. The Steeplechase had the greatest carousel I ever saw. Until I saw this one. I've got to hand it to you, Dory, it's a beauty."

The middle row of horses moved up and down in rhythm to the calliope music that streamed on currents of midnight air.

Ben reached for Dory's hand and led her down the aisle, weaving between the rows of horses, until they came to an armored carousel horse whose headstall was topped with a magnificent carved plume and whose gold-edged raiment bore the crest of some noble knight.

"My lady, if I may."

His hands encircled her waist and lifted her up onto the charger's back.

Unbidden, he jumped up behind her, his hands going around her to grasp the pole as if it were reins.

The gesture stunned Dory into speechlessness. At first, her whole body tensed at the feel of his chest, hard and firm, at her back. But the sweetly scented midnight air was like a tonic. The rhythmic prance of her beloved painted ponies in time to the gay calliope music filled her with warm memories. She smiled to herself and closed her eyes, her head falling back against his shoulder as the tension washed away and she yielded to the safety of his protective embrace.

She took refuge in what he had told her, that she could make tonight disappear with the dawn. Wants, needs, feelings, they were all that mattered when the moon was high and the night breeze rustled her hair, when the heat of his naked chest pressed against her back chased away the chill in the air, and when his strong arms were around her, not letting her fall.

Chapter 12

Dory awakened the next morning feeling something she hadn't felt in a very long time—happy.

It was a happiness seemingly without rhyme or reason, one that erased the fears that haunted her, and which went against the grain of her own logic. It made her feel giddy and not at all like herself.

Ben had told her that whatever happened between them last night could disappear with the morning's light if she wanted it to. But the sun was peeking over the treetops and slanting into her bedroom window on this brand-new day, and her skin was still flushed all over and her lips still felt raw and bruised from his kisses, and her cheek was still chafed from the rub of his stubbly chin against it.

She told herself that it had been late, that she'd been struggling with memories and hadn't known what she was doing. That she was out of her mind for opening herself up to him the way she had.

He should have known that she wasn't herself last night. How could he have used her vulnerability against her the way he had? Worse, how could she have let him?

In the state she'd been in last night, she could have believed almost anything, even that maybe he cared for her, that the pleasure he derived from her went deeper than the mere physical. She thought she had felt it in his touch, heard it in the rasp of his whisper at her ear, sensed it in the desperate way he had clung to her. Lost in the tumult of passion, she could almost have believed that he loved her, and that she loved him, and that together they could both love and share Jason.

She had even dared to wonder what it would be like to be his wife, to make him breakfast every morning and lie in his arms each night.

Yet morning shed a different light on the subject. Perhaps she had only imagined that he cared for her. After all, he had never told her he loved her. Maybe it was for the best if she just tried to pretend that nothing happened between them. The last thing she needed was to get involved again, least of all with Ben Stone.

Still, if she lived to be a hundred years old, she would never forget the tender way he had put his arm around her shoulders and held her close, and how he had not complained about the salty tears that wet his naked chest as she wept against him. There was an inherent kindness about him that touched her deeply, and she wanted him to know how much she appreciated it when she had needed it the most.

As she lay in bed during those first few minutes of awakening, she wanted to do something special for him, the way he had done something special for her last night. It would be her way of acknowledging last night without having to actually put it into words that she was still too afraid to utter. A special dinner seemed less risky, particularly since Martin and Jason would be there.

Dory got out of bed and went to the window. Raising it, she leaned out with her elbows resting on the sill, and breathed the morning air into her lungs. The sky was still hazy with the dawn. To the east lay a forest dense with oaks and sugar maples. To the west the green-carpeted Catskills gently rolled off into the horizon.

She came to this window every morning to gaze upon the scenery. Over the years she had watched the mountains perform their magic, changing from the red and burnt orange of autumn, to the white sugar frosting of winter, to the way they were now in springtime, verdant and lush and bursting with the promise of summer.

She remembered the summers of her youth, swimming in the clean, cold Neversink River, hiking through the wilderness with her father and grandfather, the chilly winter mornings when her mother would shake her awake to go to school, the crisp autumn afternoons filled with the scent of burning leaves.

She smiled, remembering the county fairs when she would sleep in the hay at night so that she could be close to Minnie, her grandfather's prize Holstein.

And through every season of her youth, there were the mountains. Year after year they were there, reassuring her with their beauty and their presence. Like her beloved carousel horses, they were her friends.

She asked herself if Ben could ever come to love

this place as much as she did. Could he ever settle down in this, her little corner of the world?

Deep in her heart, in that place where her most secret fantasies dwelled, she imagined them all living together, her, Ben, Jason and Martin, with her and Ben running the Dutch Mill and raising Jason together.

A powerful emotion came and went quickly as Dory realized just how much she wanted it to all come true.

She showered and dressed and made the bed, and was downstairs before anyone else was up, even before Martin, who was by nature an early riser. She ate a quick breakfast and hurried outside to work on the carousel. She didn't want to see Ben just yet. She needed time to think, to sort out her emotions where he was concerned.

A short while later, when the truck from the lumberyard arrived, Dory saw Ben come out of the house. While he was busy with the driver, she slipped back into the house to get Jason ready for preschool. With a kiss goodbye, she sent him off with Martin.

She should have gone back outside to work on the carousel, but she hesitated, knowing that Ben was out there. She chose instead to do some chores around the house to keep her hands busy while her mind continued to forge full steam ahead.

Should she cook a special dinner tonight, or shouldn't she? She battled with herself over it for an hour or so, until the very thought of it filled her with the same giddiness with which she had awakened.

Reaching up on tiptoe, she pulled down from the top shelf her mother's old French cookbook, still not certain that she wanted to go through with it. What if Ben misinterpreted it as something more than just her way of saying thank-you? Then again, what if it actually *was* something more?

"Was that the carousel I heard last night?"

The sound of her grandfather's voice startled Dory out of her thoughts. She kept her face averted toward the cookbook that was open on the kitchen counter so that he wouldn't see the deep blush that rose to her cheeks at the mention of last night.

Her pulse was still racing from her encounter with Ben, yet summoning a casual tone, she told him, "I was just showing Ben how it worked."

"It was kinda late to be out there, wasn't it?"

"You know me. Sometimes I have trouble sleeping, so I go out there to work on the horses."

"Was Ben having trouble sleeping, too?"

"I don't know. You'll have to ask him. All I know is, he came out there, we talked for a while, and then he asked for a ride." Neither her voice nor her manner betrayed the events that had occurred between the time he came out to the carousel and when he had asked for a ride.

Unsuspecting of what she left unsaid, he asked, "What are you doing?"

"I'm planning dinner for tonight."

He came to stand behind her, and peering over her shoulder, exclaimed, "Coq au vin? When did we turn French?"

"I thought I'd try something a little different for tonight. Where's your sense of discovery?"

"I gave it up for meat and potatoes."

"Oh, come on, you'll love it."

"Sure, but will Jason?"

"I'll cook a frankfurter for Jason."

"Hmm. Maybe I'll ask the boy if he wants to trade."

"Never mind that," she said in a scolding tone. "If you really don't want this, I can cook a frankfurter for you, too."

"I have a better idea. Why don't I take Jason out to eat tonight?"

It was then that she looked up from the recipe, alarm shooting through her at the prospect of dinner tonight alone with Ben. "But what about this delicious dinner I'm planning?"

"You and Ben have it. Jason and I will have burgers and fries."

The sly old fox. She knew what he was up to. It was his way of getting her and Ben together. What would he think if he knew just how *together* they had been last night? Blushing even harder, she turned away, and said, "Have it your way. But you're welcome to stay."

"Where is Ben this morning, anyway?"

"The lumber arrived earlier, so my guess is he's probably at the carousel, repairing the roof."

"I think I'll go out there and keep him company." He headed for the door. "Let me know when you have a list ready, and I'll drive into town."

When he was gone, Dory expelled the breath that had been trapped in her lungs. That was a close call. There was no need for Martin to know about her intimacy with Ben, at least not until she herself knew where it fit into the scheme of things and was able to come to terms with it.

That was precisely what she had been trying to do when Martin had come into the room. If he had seen her face, he would have known that she wasn't even looking at the page that had randomly fallen open to a chicken in wine recipe. If he could read her thoughts, he would have known that they had been far, far away from the room itself.

Dory glanced down haphazardly at the cookbook, and sighed. She didn't get much opportunity to cook gourmet meals. Jason was a finicky eater, preferring frankfurters, hamburgers and pizza. Martin was strictly a meat-and-potatoes man. She had no doubt that he was out there right now telling Ben about the coq au vin he was going to have that evening. She supposed she had no choice now but to go through with it.

A check of the cupboard and the refrigerator revealed that she didn't have all the ingredients the recipe called for. She quickly jotted down the missing ingredients on a piece of paper—pearl onions, mushrooms, brandy, a bottle of red wine. She brought the end of the pen to her lips and nibbled on it as she contemplated what else was needed.

Sometimes, for dessert, they had the apple pie or the peach cobbler that Mrs. Norton sent home with Jason, or the linzer tarts from the local bakery that were Martin's personal favorite.

Dory flipped through the pages of the dessert section, studying the possibilities. Then she remembered one night when she had placed some chocolate kisses on the table and Ben had devoured nearly all of them. Grinning like a schoolboy over their teasing, he had admitted to having an obsession for chocolate. Opting for a delicious-sounding chocolate mousse, she scribbled down the rest of the ingredients she needed, and then jotted down a few everyday items, hoping they would divert Martin's suspicions, yet knowing all the while that nothing ever escaped his notice.

She found him at the carousel, talking to Ben who was standing atop the ladder, hammering a piece of lumber into place.

The sound of her approach was lost in the noise of the hammering, giving Dory a few moments to observe them.

Martin was leaning back against one of the horses, merrily chatting away.

Ben wasn't saying a word. Stripped of his shirt, his upper body glistened in the rays of light that streamed in through the hole in the roof. He looked so beautiful, his muscles bursting with power, the way she remembered them from last night. His head was tilted upwards, sunlight sparkling like diamonds off the dark hair that spilled past his face.

The sight of him took Dory's breath away. But what did she expect? Since the moment she had met him, he'd had that effect on her. But it was more than his physical beauty that rendered her speechless. Last night she had discovered the kind and gentle soul beneath the masculine brawn. With a shuddering start, Dory realized that she loved him.

She swallowed hard and stepped up onto the carousel to announce her presence.

Martin came forward to greet her. "Dory," he exclaimed, gesturing around them, "I had no idea you'd accomplished so much. Fine work, my girl."

She had to raise her voice to be heard over the hammering. "I have a list for you."

He took the slip of paper from her hand and scanned it. "Hmm. Semisweet chocolate. Well, if they don't have it at Bill's Grocery, I'll just get the regular kind."

"No!" The swiftness of her response startled them both. She gave a little laugh to cover her embarrassment at having spoken so emphatically. "What I mean is, it has to be semisweet. The recipe calls for it."

With a sardonic twinkle in his eye, he asked, "What recipe is that?"

Grudgingly, she answered, "Chocolate mousse."

"More French stuff. Hmm."

"Stop sounding so suspicious."

But the smile on his weathered face as he ambled off told her that he knew she was up to something. She watched him go, thinking, if only he knew.

Caught up in her banter with Martin, Dory wasn't aware that the hammering had ceased until she turned around and saw Ben standing at the foot of the ladder.

There was a strange, unreadable look on his face and a steeliness in his eyes that rooted her to her spot. Was he displeased over her plans for dinner? Had she assumed too much?

Dory shrank inwardly at the deep, dark gaze that was focused intently upon her face. She turned to look over her shoulder, hoping to call Martin back, but with a spray of pebbles beneath its tires the car peeled off down the dirt road, and she knew it was impossible. Sucking in her breath, she turned back to Ben.

"I should have asked you if you like French food, but I—"

"I love it." He spoke in a flat, matter-of-fact monotone.

Dory felt her heart sink. Was he just being polite?

"If you would rather go with my grandfather and Jason into town, I understand."

"Damn it, Dory, why are you being so solicitous?"

She was stunned by his reaction. Perhaps he had followed his own advice and made last night disappear with the dawn. Feeling suddenly foolish for her effort, she stammered, "I just thought...I wanted you to know...that I appreciate...that is..."

"You don't have to explain it to me," he said, turning away with a disgusted look on his face.

He was visibly angry, but as she stood there feeling foolish, Dory was confused as to whom he was angry with, her or himself.

Sensing an explosive air all about him, she approached him cautiously, careful to maintain a safe distance between them. In a softly inquisitive voice she asked, "Ben, are you angry with me?"

Ben closed his eyes in anguish. He could never be angry with her, not when she had filled the hole inside of him last night that he had needed so desperately to be filled.

He had lain awake the rest of the night, thinking about their encounter at the carousel and the terrible need it aroused in him. He had tried to tell himself that he wanted her because she was there. Icing on the cake, so to speak. What man in his right mind *wouldn't* want her? It wasn't his lust for her that scared him, though. What scared him most was that even as his mouth had been on hers, his hands closing around that firm, female flesh, he had known it came down to more than mere physical desire.

Lots of women had smooth skin and soft lips, and after all, arousal came easily to a man who had spent three years in only the company of other men. But what he felt for this particular woman went beyond the basic instinct to couple. It was more than just her beautiful face and alluring smile. There was an essence about her, a special kind of magic that came from her being simply who she was, and that essence somehow quelled his fears. What he felt for her was want and need combined until he could not tell where one emotion began and the other ended. It was her he wanted, with her sea-green eyes sparkling with intelligence, her smile giving him hope, her body offering him forgiveness for the sins of his past.

He had lain awake in bed all night, trying to sort it all out. Dory, Jason, his feelings for them both, and where, if anywhere at all, he fit in. It was the same thing he had asked himself countless times before. Only last night had been different. With the coming of dawn, something had changed. The old feelings of pain and bitterness were still there. The physical need he had for Dory was as strong and overwhelming as ever.

He craved the feel of her, the scent of her, the way her hands drove him wild with anticipation. He admired her beauty and her intelligence. But most of all, he admired her courage. She could not have felt any less afraid and vulnerable last night when she told him about Eddie and the fire than he did right now. In the face of that quiet courage, how could he offer her any less?

He turned to look into her frightened eyes. Softly, he said, "No, Dory, I'm not angry with you. It's myself I'm angry at."

Taking it as self-reproach, Dory groaned inwardly, fearing the worst, that he was angry at himself for the weakness that had led him to make love to her.

"Ben, I understand if you're sorry it happened." She blushed deeply and lowered her lashes, unable to look him in the eyes as her voice dropped to almost a whisper. "You know, making love."

"Is that what you think? That I'm sorry it happened?"

Her gaze returned to his, confused and questioning. "I thought that's what you're angry about, that you regret it."

"Regret making love to you? God, no. Dory, I've never experienced anything like last night. You were incredible, so loving and giving. You made me feel whole, like the part of me that had been missing before last night was suddenly restored. I want you, more than I've ever wanted any woman. I'd be a liar to deny it. But I don't deserve you. Not when I've been less than truthful with you."

"Less than truthful about what?"

Last night he had felt closer to her than he had ever felt to any other human being. Yet as much as he wanted to say it, the words stuck like glue to his tongue. He thought again about the courage it had taken for her to reveal her painful secrets and regrets, and drawing in a ragged breath, he said in a low, plaintive voice, "There's something I must tell you."

Dory's whole body went rigid with fear. "Th-there's more? About Jason?"

"No, it's not about Jason. It's about me. It's about my past."

"You were an architect. You made a lot of money. You lived in Manhattan. You had a bad divorce."

She recited aloud the facts she knew about his past, while inwardly her thoughts collided. What could it be? What could be so terrible that it put that look of fear in his dark eyes and the tremor in his voice?

He placed the hammer down, picked up his shirt and put it on, then went to sit on the edge of the carousel. He glanced around at the horses on either side of him. This was the very spot where Dory had revealed her secret pain to him late last night. Sitting there in the bright light of day, Ben knew that he could not feel the things he felt for her and not be totally honest with her. His own moment of truth had arrived.

Chapter 13

The atmosphere was filled with a charged silence as Ben grappled with the words.

Taking in a deep breath, he let it out slowly through pursed lips and said solemnly, "Nothing gets better when you keep it in, does it?"

He had become a pro at keeping things inside, sometimes not even acknowledging them to himself. How could he ever expect her to forgive him for his past when he had not learned to forgive himself? The crusty layers of anger and bitterness that had built up over the years hid the soft, vulnerable underside of his emotions, only adding to his fear of believing that any kind of happiness could come to a man like him. It was only the hope that he had found his son that kept him going from day to day. Only the growing feelings that Dory stirred in him that gave him the courage to tell his story.

Dory's own fears were swiftly overshadowed by the

ones she saw reflected on Ben's handsome face. In a hushed voice, she replied, "I guess that's something we both know about."

Ben didn't know if it was the quiet understanding he saw in her eyes, telling him that she knew what it was like to be lonely and afraid, or the soft, reassuring sound of her voice, or the touch of her hand ever so lightly on his shoulder, telling him that he wasn't alone, that brought the words kept too long unspoken.

A muscle twitched at the corner of his mouth, pulling it downward into a frown as he began to speak. His voice was low and unsteady.

"My wife was the daughter of an orthopedic surgeon. She grew up on Central Park West in a ten-room apartment that cost almost as much per month as some people earn in a year. I was a junior partner in an architectural firm when we met. By the time we got married, I'd been made a full partner. We were a perfect match. The more money I made, the more money she spent. It actually worked for a while."

He drifted into silent remembering of the early years of his marriage, when he'd been ambitious to succeed and too naive to know where it would all lead.

"What happened?"

Dory's soft-spoken voice called him back to the present. "What usually happens?" he said dully. "Someone changes. And suddenly, your whole world changes. Your world changed when Eddie started drinking. Mine changed when Allison started fooling around."

He gave a derisive little snort at the irony of the past. "It's funny, but like you, I actually blamed myself at first. I was working a lot at the time, putting in long hours on-site and at the office. I knew she was lonely, but hell, so was I.''

Glancing at Dory from time to time as he spoke, he saw no sign of the hatred or revulsion that he knew would come later. On the contrary, the expression on her face was one of empathy and understanding.

The words came quicker now, and easier. "I didn't do it for myself. I did it for us. What I didn't know at the time was that 'us' included all of Allison's boyfriends. First it was one guy, then it was another. A beautiful woman with money to toss around is a target for every opportunistic creep that comes around. They just naturally gravitated toward her. But I soon discovered Allison changed boyfriends as easily as she changed clothes. I realized I was out there busting my butt for nothing.''

Dory shook her head with sad understanding. "It's incredible, the things we don't see when we *think* we're in love.''

"That's it,'' he said. "That's exactly the way it was with me. Okay, so I admit it, I married Allison for all the wrong reasons. She was beautiful and ambitious and I thought I loved her. It's funny what you can mistake for love.''

Dory looked off into the distance, recalling what she had mistaken for love. "Sometimes, you can want something so bad that you find yourself living more for the fantasy you've created in your mind than the reality around you. Then, when things go wrong, you tell yourself that it must be your fault.'' She looked back at him, her brows knit with concern. "But Ben, surely you don't blame yourself for her infidelities.''

"I don't know, Dory. You know how you said that sometimes you feel if you'd somehow been different, things wouldn't have gone wrong between you and Eddie? Well, that's the way it is with me. Sometimes I can't help but think that the way things ultimately turned out might have been avoided if I'd been there more for her.''

She could have no idea that the way things had turned out for Ben included something far worse than divorce. Thinking that he was still hurting over the demise of his marriage, she tried to make him feel better by placing the blame where it rightfully belonged.

''I don't care what her reasons were for being unfaithful to you. When you love someone, I mean when you *truly* love someone, how can you even *think* of it? If I had that kind of love and commitment from a man, I'd consider myself the luckiest woman on the face of the earth.''

And if that man were Ben Stone, she would have shared anything with him, even her son. But she didn't say that.

''Allison had something that most women dream of,'' she told him. ''A husband who loved her and took care of her. That she could scoff in the face of that love is something I'll never understand.''

''I know now that Allison never truly loved me, nor I her. We were a flashy couple. We went to all the right parties and gallery openings and met all the right people in our rise to the top...or should I say, in *my* rise to the top and Allison's ride along. But flash doesn't last very long. We had maybe two good years before things went sour. When I found out about her extracurricular activities, we separated. Still, I figured, who knows, if I could get her to stop running around, maybe there was a chance of saving the marriage after all. So, I called her bluff. I told her that if she didn't stop running around, I'd divorce her and cut her off without a penny.''

His expression turned unreadable as the memories of that dark time flooded back to him.

''I assume from the look on your face,'' said Dory, ''that the threat didn't work.''

He shook his head at the cruel humor of it. ''It backfired right in my face. But even then, I didn't realize the lengths to which she would go to protect her own interests.'' He laughed, but it was a bitter sound from deep in his throat. ''And they say that hell hath no fury like a woman scorned. How about the one who's looking to take you to the cleaners, financially as well as emotionally?''

''You must have lost big in the divorce.''

''Oh, I lost big, all right. Bigger than you can ever imagine.''

She had been referring to the money he must have lost in the divorce settlement, but she could tell from the look on his face that he had lost much more than that. She assumed that, like herself, he had lost his faith in love and commitment and in his own judgment.

In a consoling tone, she said to him, ''I know the feeling.''

He looked up at her. She was standing before him, silhouetted by sunlight, her chestnut hair sparkling like a halo all around her. He knew by the unrestrained outline of her nipples beneath her T-shirt that she wasn't wearing a bra. Her natural beauty and uncontrived sexiness was so different from what he had known before. She had become precious and necessary to him, something he needed as much as the air he breathed.

"Does it ever go away?" he asked.

"I used to think it never would."

His eyes gently pleaded with hers. "And now?"

She knew what he wanted to hear, that with his help her faith had been restored, yet she was reluctant to admit it, even to herself, except to say, "I think it might be possible."

But Dory reminded herself that faith in love was not the only thing Ben had lost. There was also the son his wife had given up for adoption. She didn't know if a hurt like that could ever really go away.

She thought she understood now why he had chosen a drifter's life-style free of entanglements and attachments, and why it was so important to him for Jason to be his son. In a way, she wished that Jason were Ben's son. Maybe then this problem between them would be resolved, and the terrible pain he must be feeling might be laid to rest.

Her heart went out to him. "It must have been very difficult for you when you learned about your son."

"Loneliness," he muttered, "It makes fools of us all."

He told her then about the Christmas Eve Allison had knocked on his door, how his lonely need had driven him into her arms one last time, and how, unable to bear her constant demands for more money, he had gone to her apartment several months later to have it out with her and had found her pregnant.

"Are you sure the child was yours?" Dory asked, knowing that he must have asked himself the very same thing.

"It was mine. She made sure of it. It was all part of the plan."

He ran his hand through his hair, sweeping the dark locks from his eyes with a tired gesture. His voice sounded weary, like that of a man who had been through it all in his own mind a thousand times without any easy answers.

"In retrospect, it isn't hard to figure out her motives. She'd become accustomed to spending freely. A divorce would have meant a change in life-style. To ensure against that happening, she manipulated me into getting her pregnant. You see, she planned all along on putting the baby up for adoption to make some money."

He heard Dory's muffled gasp. "I know what you're thinking," he said. "How could she do it?" He answered his own question with a contemptuous snort. "Hell, how do I know why Allison did anything? At heart, she wasn't a bad person, not really. She did what she felt she had to do to get by, just like we all do what we have to do when we get right down to it. Of course, I wasn't feeling quite so charitable toward her at the time. But then, I've had a lot of time to think about it."

"If her father was wealthy, couldn't she have gone to him for money?" Dory questioned.

"She probably did. But the old guy was tough. He grew up on the lower east side of Manhattan, having to steal coal from the coal wagons. He put himself through medical school at night while working two jobs. She told me once that when she was growing up, she got less allowance than the daughter of their maid. No doubt he looked unfavorably on her life-style, and wasn't about to subsidize it."

"I can understand giving up a child to give it a chance at a better life, but for *money?* Oh, Ben, how that must have hurt you. Did you confront her about it?"

"No, I didn't."

"But you had every right to tell her exactly what you thought of the terrible thing she did."

"I couldn't do that. By the time I found out about the baby and the adoption, she was dead." He paused to take a deep breath, and added soberly, "She was murdered."

He let the air out of his lungs in one long, low whoosh, and dropped his head into his hands. "God help me, but I hated her so much at the time, I wanted to kill her."

He didn't see Dory's mouth drop open nor her eyes widen with disbelief.

Murdered? No, it wasn't possible. Ben wasn't capable of violence. Living in such close proximity these past weeks, wouldn't she have sensed a violent nature, or felt it in his touch? So, maybe he had wanted to kill her, but he didn't actually do it. Or did he?

Eddie's image sprang into her mind. She hadn't sensed it in him either, not at the beginning. No, she cried silently, it was impossible that there could be any similarities between them.

"How did she...I mean, who..."

"She was shot by a jealous lover. The neighbors heard them arguing. One of them saw the guy run out of the building and later identified him in a lineup."

She sat down beside him on the edge of the carousel, feeling weak with relief knowing that he wasn't guilty of the terrible crime. "You told me once that you weren't around when she put your child up for adoption. Where were you?''

Ben winced, for they were headed into dangerous water. He turned to face her and looked strongly into her beautiful eyes. ''That brings me to what I wanted to tell you.''

There was something odd in his gaze, something Dory had never seen before. She felt an inexplicable apprehension wash over her.

''I never confronted Allison about the adoption because I didn't know about it. And the reason I didn't know about it was because I was in prison.''

Dory stared back blankly, as if he were speaking a foreign language.

''Dory? Did you hear me? I said—''

''I heard you.'' Her ragged whisper sliced right through his words. ''Prison?'' She repeated the word, as if uttering it aloud would somehow make sense out of it. ''But you said it was a jealous lover who killed her.''

He swallowed hard in an attempt to dislodge the lump that had formed in his throat. He knew there was no easy way to tell her what he also knew he must.

''That's not what they put me away for. I was arrested, tried and convicted for beating her. I spent three years in prison for assault.''

He braced himself for her reaction. Shock. Outrage. Hatred. Revulsion. Anything would have been better than the look he saw on her face. It was an expression of utter hopelessness, as if the one thing she had depended upon in the world, hope, was suddenly shattered.

Dory felt her extremities turn cold first, and then numb with disbelief as the words sank slowly into her brain, each one killing her a little more than the one before it.

She was not cognizant of the tears that sprang from her eyes without warning, nor of jumping to her feet and running away from him as fast as she could.

Her heart pounded savagely in her chest, threatening to explode. She ran blindly into the woods, hot tears obscuring her vision, the sharp thorns of the bushes snagging her jeans and pricking her skin as she thrashed through them. She ran until she was breathless and could not run anymore. And then she collapsed on the ground, weeping inconsolably.

It was shocking to think that she didn't really know him at all. It wasn't even the thought of prison that upset her so much. It was the awful realization that she was falling for a man whom she couldn't trust—a man who could potentially threaten her relationship with Jason and shatter her own resolve to never fall in love again.

She had heard the desolation in his voice. Lurking behind the words she had sensed his lack of belief in love, and it had stunned her. She had sworn to herself a long time ago that she would not get involved with a man incapable of love again. She had avoided love for that very reason, sacrificing the chance to fulfill her dreams in favor of safety for herself and her son.

Yet it seemed now that all the feelings of safety and protection that she had felt in Ben's arms last night had been nothing more than her own desperate imagination. How could there be safety in the arms of a man she didn't know?

Through the tears that blinded her vision one thing

seemed clear. Ben was only sticking around because of Jason, and if Jason was not his son, he would disappear from her life forever.

Chapter 14

He found her crumpled in a small heap at the base of a tree, her head cradled in her arms, weeping softly. He dropped to one knee beside her and placed a hand on her shoulder.

"Dory, please, let me explain."

She rolled over and jerked away from him as if she'd been struck by lightning. "Don't touch me!"

In her tear-bright eyes Ben saw her mistrust and suspicion, and something else that turned his blood cold. It was her fear of him.

Something inside of him hardened like stone at the realization that the understanding and lack of recrimination he had hoped for would not be forthcoming.

"Damn it, Dory, why are you so quick to judge me?"

She edged away from him and remained with her back pressed against the trunk of the tree, looking like a frightened, cornered creature.

"I expected some kind of reaction from you, but not a guilty verdict, not without even hearing all the facts."

His anger was rapidly mounting, for suddenly he found himself having to defend his innocence all over again, only this time to a woman who had somehow come to mean too much to him.

"The least you can do is hear me out, damn it. And if you think I'm the devil incarnate after that, then so be it. I'll leave, for good, without Jason. You can be the judge and jury, Dory, but you've got to hear me out."

With that part about leaving without Jason, Dory was more than ever determined not to believe anything he said. "What can you possibly say to me that would make any difference?" she shot back at him. "Maybe if I hadn't had that kind of husband myself, I might be able to summon some remote understanding for you, but for God's sake, Ben, what kind of fool do you take me for?"

"But that's just it," he said, his voice rising. "I wasn't that kind of husband. I'm telling you, Dory, I didn't do it. How could you think that I could?"

He sounded genuinely hurt that she could believe such a thing of him. Confused, she stammered, "You—you said they arrested you for it. You said there was a trial and a conviction."

"Don't you see, Dory? She lied on the witness stand. She named me as her attacker because she knew that if I was behind bars, I'd never be able to stop the adoption. I was the only thing standing in her way, so she found a way to get rid of me."

"Are you suggesting that she somehow beat herself

up, or that she hired someone to do it just so that she could blame it on you?"

He stiffened at the sarcastic barb, for in her sharp tone he heard her disbelief. "Of course not. I didn't know at the time who did it. I found out later it was the same guy who killed her. If I had known then what I know now, I would have killed him with my bare hands. Allison and I didn't get along very well at the end, and she could be real devious at times, but she didn't deserve the beating that guy gave her. Maybe he found out that she was trading him in for someone else and didn't like the idea. Man, you should have seen her. It was hard to imagine that there was a beautiful face beneath all those bruises. I could almost have felt sorry for her." His tone hardened like steel when he added, "Except for the fact that she told the cops it was me who did it."

In the quiet of the morning, surrounded by mountains and woodland, far from where it had all occurred, in a low voice that cracked at times with emotion, he told her about the trial.

"She sat on that witness stand, looking so pathetic with her bruises and her tears, and when they asked her if the person who did that to her was in the courtroom, she said yes and pointed to me. God, how she must have hated me."

"And they believed her?" Dory's voice sounded small and unsure compared to the enormity of what she was hearing.

"They fell for it hook, line and sinker. And I got five years behind bars."

"I thought you said you spent three years in prison."

"Yeah, lucky me. I was pardoned after three years

when the guy who murdered her confessed to the assault as part of his plea bargain.''

Dory sank back down against the tree, her mind spinning out of control as she struggled with this latest revelation.

He went on in the same low, bitter tone. ''She came to visit me one day in prison. It was the only time she did. It was to bring me the divorce papers to sign. By then, she'd had the baby. When I asked about it, she told me she'd given it up for adoption.''

His face retained its stoic expression, but his ebony eyes blazed with acrimony. ''I thought I'd been hit with a bullet. When the shock wore off, I wanted to break through the glass that separates the inmates from the visitors and rip that phone out of her ringed fingers and kill her for what she'd done. But there was nothing I could do. A few days later she was dead. And soon after that I was a free man.''

''How did you know that Celina Bonham had handled the adoption?'' Dory asked.

''I found out during Allison's visit. You should have seen her. She looked so beautiful and so vengeful in her triumph. It must have satisfied some perverse need she had to deepen my pain by telling me about the adoption. She got a little too cocky about it and made the mistake of telling me the name of the attorney. The first thing I did when I was released was go to see Celina Bonham, only to learn that I had terminated my parental rights by not coming forward to contest the adoption within the first six months.''

Dory felt an overwhelming wave of guilt wash over her for having misjudged him, yet at the same time she was afraid to believe him, and even more afraid to trust him.

"So, that's what the attorney meant when she referred to the circumstances of your case. But surely, under such bizarre circumstances—"

"The courts don't give a damn about circumstances," he cut in, guessing her intention. "I learned that the hard way. If it hadn't been for some mousey little clerk in the attorney's office, who just happened to read something aloud from the file in my presence, I never would have known where to begin to search for my son."

He could read the uncertainty in Dory's eyes and feel it in the way she shrank from him. If there was anything worse for him than everything that had come before, it was her not believing him now. Inching closer to her, yet careful not to touch her, he searched her face with a beseeching expression, begging her with his eyes not to judge him too harshly, and most of all, not to hate him.

"God knows, I've made mistakes in my life. But I'm no wife beater. You believe me, don't you, Dory?"

She turned her tear-stained face away. Her silence was palpable.

Ben's throat went dry, and for the first time in a long time he was truly scared. "Look at me," he begged. "Look at me and tell me you believe me."

Dory closed her eyes in anguish. "Oh, Ben, I don't know what to believe anymore."

The hope in his eyes died and his voice softened to something that sounded like helplessness. "I want to try to work things out with you, but I don't know how. I can see that you're trying hard to get your life back in order for your sake and for Jason's. And with my own bad experience behind me, I can understand your reluctance to get involved with someone like me. But that doesn't mean I can just walk away from what we've started here—'' He paused, reluctant to even discuss the feelings that had sprung up between them. He continued, amending his words. ''I can't walk away from Jason.''

His head was filled with all the unspoken thoughts, such as how he yearned for her and wanted desperately to be a part of the relationship between her and Jason, and how he knew that, in the end, it was all up to her.

Dory became even more frightened and confused. What if they found out that Jason was not his son? Would that be the end? She longed to hear him tell her that he loved her, and now a part of her could not help but wonder if he would walk away if Jason was not his son.

''I need time to think,'' she said. ''I have to consider everything.''

''Think all you want,'' he told her. ''Just don't forget to consider this.''

This time when he took her into his arms, it was not merely to comfort her as it had been the first time, but to take for himself the comfort which, ironically, only she was able to give him.

His breath was warm against the side of her face. ''I need you, Dory.''

She was torn by two impulses. If she stayed, she would be beyond saving. If she ran away, she would never know the truth of whether he could ever love her.

Up until last night, every time she had felt him getting too close, her defenses had slammed on the brakes. Where were her defenses last night when it mattered, and where were they now when, in spite of everything, she moved easily into his embrace?

She felt her muscles go weak as he caressed the back of her neck and splayed his strong fingers in her hair. One last shred of defense warned her that she'd better back away. She knew where this was heading. They both knew. Certain things didn't have to be said.

He had told her that he needed her, and the words still left an empty space within her that was filled with doubt and uncertainty. Maybe need would be enough.

Need was different. Her own need came from a place so deep down inside that it had to be dragged kicking and screaming to the surface. The fulfillment of that need last night in his arms was potent and powerful, for it encompassed everything that was necessary for her survival.

They were both kneeling on the ground, facing each other. In Ben's hot, ardent gaze Dory recognized his need. All thoughts of a special dinner had vanished from her mind long before this moment. This, she thought, as she yielded to his need, this was how she would show him how much she appreciated what he had done for her last night.

Ben's breath caught in his throat when Dory's fingers slid up his chest and began to unbutton his denim shirt. His flesh burned at the brush of her silken hands as each button came undone.

She pushed the shirt from his shoulders and watched as he did the rest, pulling it out of his jeans and tossing it aside to reveal more of his beautiful masculine form to her eager eyes.

When he was stripped to the waist, she rose fluidly to her feet. Standing before his kneeling form, she began slowly to undress.

Her body was beautiful in the sunlight that slanted through the branches of the trees. The bare skin of her shoulders looked even paler compared to the rich, deep darkness of her hair. He longed to crush the silky tresses in his fingers, but he held himself in check, so mesmerized was he by the sight of her that he was helpless to do anything except stare at her.

She stepped out of her jeans and left them in a soft heap on the ground. She heard his quick intake of breath when she came forward and took his hand in hers and pulled him gently to the ground beside her.

His whole body went rigid when her fingers moved to the zipper of his jeans and he moaned audibly when a slender, white hand slipped inside to grasp him.

She felt a surge of blood through her veins at the sheer power of him and the incredible heat that burned beneath her touch. She had an overwhelming ache for his power, his strength. She wanted to hold it, to taste it, to feel it inside of her. She could have lain back and opened herself up to him and let him fill her aching body and her need all at the same time. But this was no longer about her need. It was about his.

She melted against him, dark lashes fluttering closed, lips parting to rain feather-soft kisses across his naked chest. The tip of her tongue brushed his nipples, tickling them into hardness, before moving downward to savor the taut skin at his stomach.

His breath was coming in short, hard bursts through his nostrils as she slid his jeans down past his slim hips. He tangled his fingers in her hair as her dark head moved with torturous intent to that place that throbbed for her. She was driving him wild with her kisses, but it was a sweet kind of torture, one he would gladly die of. But no such relief was in store for him.

The pressure mounted. When he was on the verge of exploding, he grasped her by the shoulders, fingers biting into her flesh with unintentioned hardness, and pulled her face back up to his.

He kissed her hard, devouring her with all the craving that was in him, while his hands sought the soft, giving flesh of her breasts, the firmness of her nipples straining against his palms.

Last night, in the dark, he had gotten only a glimpse of her smooth, firm flesh by moonlight. But here beneath the trees, in the diffused light of day, he saw her clearly. Her eyes were closed, but his were open, devouring every inch of her beauty and committing it all to memory.

His touch moved over her bare breasts, cupping, lifting, caressing, teasing, stroking their soft, sensitive undersides, thumbs working in slow, seductive harmony over her nipples. She sucked in her breath when his hands slid to the hollow of her waist and glided like skaters on ice to the swell of her hips. She could feel the scrape of his calluses against her buttocks when he cupped them tightly and pulled her up against his swollen arousal.

She had wanted to satisfy his need, and somehow he was satisfying hers, and she realized with some detached part of her mind that their needs were one.

She was overwhelmed by the strong, flavorful taste of him on her lips, the scent of him, hot and sexual, the sound of his breath ragged at her ear, and though she wanted to experience each individual sensation and luxuriate in every stroke of his fingers and flick of his tongue, she was unable to go slow, feeling instead like a comet hurtling through the sky.

When his fingers sought that place that burned like

a wildfire out of control, it was only the sound of her moan and the press of her body against his hand that made him linger.

One slender ray of sunlight fell upon her breast, illuminating the flawless skin, guiding the way for his mouth to seek the hardened little peak that strained upwards, inviting him. He took it into his mouth and kissed it deeply, fully, seeking its nourishment the way a starving man seeks sustenance, knowing that, at the moment, it was the only thing keeping him alive.

Her skin was hot and somehow even softer with the heat. Her scent seemed intensified from it. Mingling with the smell of the earth and the leaves, it created a raw, primitive urge that threatened his self-control.

She twisted provocatively beneath him, her mouth hot and persuasive under his, insisting *yes, yes,* and inviting him to possess her fully.

In the end, caught up in a whirlwind of unstoppable passion, they both abandoned any attempt to go slowly. They clung to each other, tumbling about on their carpet of crushed grass, arms and legs entangled, mouths melded together, tongues meeting, breath mingling.

Her own passion out of control, Dory sensed his need and matched it with her own. It was basic and elemental and so very necessary. "Ben," she whispered, her fingers entwining in his thick dark hair, "make love to me. Now, Ben. Now..."

She was open and ready for him, lips parted, legs widening, arms embracing. He surged into her, his lean, limber body answering her heated demands.

Passion and energy raced unchecked between them. She kissed him and touched him and weakened him. She demanded when he expected surrender, thrilling him in a way he had thought existed only in a man's wildest fantasies. But this was no fantasy. This was real and it was honest. Their need was not just of the flesh; it was for each other.

The feel of him filling her, taking her higher and higher until she craved sweet release, was unlike anything Dory had ever experienced. What had begun as a tender effort on her part to satisfy his longings had turned into a wild symphony resounding throughout her entire being. She closed herself around him, pulling him deeper into her sweet, moist softness, and with her own pulse thundering in her ears, she loved him back with a desperate hunger of her own.

The spring air evaporated the perspiration from their bodies, and the cadence of their breathing gradually returned to normal as they lay on the ground in each other's arms. Overhead, a canopy of leaves shielded them from the bright sun that was inching higher in the clear blue sky. One random ray broke through to illuminate the velvety moss at the base of the tree beneath which they lay. Birds chirped unseen in the branches while butterflies flitted about, going from one wildflower to another.

Dory felt strangely content in the wake of their lovemaking. It was as if something had been settled between them. There was no need for pretenses any longer. No more excuses. The attraction that had existed between them from the moment they met had been acknowledged and satisfied in a way she'd never thought possible.

He had made love to her as if she were the only woman in the world. He had not only taken, but he had given, making her pleasure as complete as his own. He was a paradox, a man capable of taking from her the thing she loved the most, yet at the same time, giving her the thing she needed most. In his arms she felt renewed.

She nestled in the crook of his arm, her dark hair spilling across his shoulder, feeling warm and protected and a million miles away from everything which, not so very long ago, had troubled her. She stirred, stretching like a kitten in the grass, and raised her eyes to look at him.

He seemed to be a million miles away, and although his expression was thoughtful, it showed no sign of regret. For that she was glad.

Her fantasies about him had proven accurate. He wasn't an easy lover. He demanded and took as much as he gave with a fierceness that frightened her, for she knew the depths from which it came.

She didn't want to think about the real world that waited for her in the clearing. Or the painful issue still at hand. Or the fact that, in spite of everything, there still lurked the tiniest bit of doubt in her mind.

He had spoken so emotionally about the son he'd never seen. At times, even though his voice had been scarcely a whisper, she'd been chilled to the bone by its ominous ring. He was a man determined to have a child of his own, that much was evident. The question that hovered in Dory's mind as she lay snuggled against him in the warm spring sunshine was whether or not he would still be around if that child wasn't Jason.

Not wishing to say anything that would break the spell of the moment, and pushing her own misgivings aside, she asked, "What are you thinking?"

He ceased the lazy pattern he was tracing over her

skin with the tip of his finger. "To tell you the truth, I was trying not to think."

"Is it working?"

"No, not really. I used to be good at it, though, in prison."

Dory shuddered against him. "It must have been so horrible."

"It was like there was this little switch inside of me that I could flip to shut off my brain. I worked, I ate, I slept. The next morning I got up and worked and ate and slept again. Life became a series of mechanical maneuvers. There was no need to even think about it. Of course, then there were the times when the switch was stuck in the on position. That's when things got really rough. There you are in this tiny, caged space, just you and your thoughts to drive you crazy."

He rolled away from her and sat up, and she could feel the unmistakable bite of tension in the air. Some wounds never healed, and she suspected that the ones he had sustained to his heart and his mind in prison would stay with him always.

"I'm sorry for the way I reacted without hearing you out," she said. "Who am I to judge you?"

He ran the back of his finger tenderly across her cheek. "You don't have to apologize to me for that. You had every right to react the way you did. And as far as judging me, hell, Dory, that only makes you human. We like to think we're better than that, but sometimes we just can't help ourselves."

Like the way he couldn't help himself from wanting her all over again, not just for the incredible pleasure of her body, but for the comfort he found in it. He might never be able to shout it to the rest of the world, but in the quiet of the woods, he had spoken to her about his memories, confiding only to her the pain and frustration of the past five years.

To speak of it had somehow freed him. The memories would always be there; like the scars of a battle wound, they were a part of him now. But for the first time he felt that he could live with them.

With her cheek still tingling from his touch, Dory rose and went in search of her clothes. She dressed with her back to him, knowing that he was watching her, and blushing with embarrassment even though he had already done so much more than look.

"We should be getting back," she said.

With those few words reality hit Ben like a bucket of cold water. He had taken a chance in opening himself up like he had, risking not only his future with his son, but any chance at happiness with Dory.

What was he thinking? What happiness could there be with Dory when he was incapable of giving her the love she needed and deserved? She deserved so much more than the basic coupling he could provide. Despite the passion that had raced unchecked between them only minutes ago, in the wake of their lovemaking, he was feeling just as much the loner as ever, just as destined to live without love in his life. Having lost almost everything because of his past, he saw little hope in the future.

He pulled his jeans up over his slim flanks, wondering yet again if there was any place for him in her life.

He shrugged into his denim shirt, pushing the sleeves up past his elbows as he followed Dory out of the woods.

Back at the carousel, Dory cast a quick glance around. The car wasn't there. Thank goodness Martin wouldn't be back for a while. She would have had a heck of a time explaining the disarray of her hair and the smell of crushed grass that clung to her.

"I have to go back to the house," she said nervously. "You can just do whatever it was you were doing."

"The roof. I was repairing the roof."

"Right." She turned to go, wanting to say more, but not knowing what.

"Dory?"

She turned back, her heart beating a little faster. "Yes?"

"Are you still going to make that special dinner Martin was telling me about?"

"Oh, the dinner." She had completely forgotten. "Why, yes. I mean, sure. That is, if you still want it."

"Yeah," he said. "I do."

Inside, her heart was tripping over itself. "Martin and Jason won't be there."

"I know."

She wet her lips. "All right."

But neither of them moved.

In a ragged breath, he urged, "You'd better go. Because if you don't, I may not be able to wait until dinner to have something to eat."

Dory's eyes flew open, partly out of shock, but mostly from pure delight. The thought of being devoured by him like some deliciously sweet dessert sent shivers down her spine. It was only the sound of approaching tires on the dirt road that prevented her from responding to it and sent her hurrying back to the house.

Chapter 15

The kitchen was bathed in the dim yellow glow of the overhead light and scented with the aroma of bread browning in the oven.

The table was set for two. Candles burned in cut-crystal holders atop a pretty tablecloth of Brussels lace that had belonged to her mother.

Dory bit her bottom lip nervously, wondering if the effect was too romantic. Twice she blew out the candles, only to light them again.

She felt like a schoolgirl on a first date, hands fumbling, her breathing slightly erratic as she hummed nervously to herself, checking and re-checking everything, including her own reflection in the glass of the cabinet door.

It was silly to think that this was a date, she told herself. Yet she could not deny that it had all the earmarks of one—the sweaty palms, the nervous sweeping aside of the dark locks that curved toward her face, the continuous wetting of her lips that were anxious with anticipation.

She was grateful that Martin had the wherewithal to sense what was going on, and the decency to not embarrass her by mentioning it, although she had suffered the sarcastic questioning that afternoon about the dinner she was planning, and a bemused look on his face a short while ago when he and Jason left to go into town.

"Why aren't you and Ben coming with me and Pop-Pop, Mommy?" her son had asked her, and she hadn't known how to respond to him.

Her inability to answer was due partly because she knew of no way to explain it to a four-year-old, but mostly because of the way he had said it. *You and Ben.* All in the same breath, as if they were one thing. It had sounded so right that it stunned her.

As she moved about the kitchen, she repeated it to herself, slowly first, then faster, until the words ran together in her mind to form a single sound, a hum that reverberated through her entire being.

She imagined that this must be what it was like to live with him, not just as boarder and employer, which, in reality, was what they were, but as, well, husband and wife, for instance. She would cook his breakfasts and sometimes make a special dinner. Certainly not extravagant gestures, but it was, after all, the little things that meant the most. At night she would sleep beside him, safe and secure, reduced to unspeakable pleasure by his lovemaking. And together, they would love Jason.

More and more Dory's thoughts turned toward her family, and the deep, abiding love she had for her grandfather and her son. But there was someone else she had come to love just as strongly. In her mind she could even picture him around the house, doing the things that she imagined a man of the house would do, like fixing leaking faucets and building tree houses.

She couldn't pinpoint precisely when she had begun to think of Ben that way, although she knew the exact moment she had fallen in love with him.

It was the night she had stood in the doorway to his room and observed him with her son. There had been a tender awkwardness about him, as if he had no clue how to relate to a four-year-old. In retrospect, his nervousness was understandable, knowing that he hadn't spent much time around children before meeting Jason.

Yet despite the awkwardness she had sensed from the doorway, he had exhibited a warmheartedness toward Jason that had touched her, and in that moment, she knew she loved him.

She remembered thinking that a man who could display such gentleness and sensitivity toward a child would make a good father. Now she wondered whether the tender feelings she saw him display toward her son were more than just those of a man being nice to a precocious child, or whether, more likely, he had already begun to suspect that Jason was his.

And it wasn't until much later that Dory had begun to suspect it, as well. It was funny, but the prospect no longer terrified her as it had in those first days and weeks of discovery. Perhaps it was knowing what she knew about him, the tragedy and trials he had endured, or the wild heights of passion he lifted her to, or the fact that she had come to love him with every desperate craving in her soul. But the fear was gone. Now, the only thing Dory feared was losing him.

But it wasn't just her feelings for him that had changed over the last few weeks. Somewhere along the way she had begun to think of Ben as Jason's father. It began with the trip to the attorney's office, when the stark legality of it hit her. Prior to that, she had reacted solely with emotion. But that afternoon, sitting in the stiff-backed chair before the attorney's desk, she'd had to deal for the first time with the very real possibility that Ben was Jason's father.

That's when her mind had taken over, trying to come up with ways to deal with the situation. She had analyzed it from every possible angle, considering everything that might or could happen. Or so she thought. One thing she had never considered was that she might fall in love with him. And what good did that do? she asked herself. She wasn't at all certain of his feelings for her or what future there could be with a man who couldn't love.

She wasn't aware that her movements had come to a halt as she contemplated the crazy turn her life had taken. She stood motionless, filled for the first time with a sense of hope.

"Regrets, green eyes?"

Dory whirled around to the deep timbre of Ben's voice from behind. He was standing in the doorway as calm as could be. He was wearing what looked to be a new pair of jeans that were slung a little low on his hips. The sleeves of a shirt she'd never seen him wearing before spanned the muscles of his upper arms, which were folded across his chest.

Dory lowered her gaze shyly, and admitted, "No. No regrets."

He came forward and caught her under the chin with the tip of his forefinger and guided her face toward his. "I've dreamed of you like this," he whispered.

She blushed furiously.

"That's not what I meant," he said with a soft chuckle. "Although, to be perfectly honest with you, I wanted to make love to you the minute I saw you. No, I meant here, in the kitchen."

"The dining room's a mess," she said apologetically. "Jason's toys are all over the place. I didn't think you'd mind eating in the kitchen."

"No, it's perfect. I like it like this, just you and me, here in the kitchen, doing the kind of things that most…" He caught himself in the nick of time about to say "married people do," and made a simple transition to "…that most people do."

He had come to love this kind of life, the straight-forward simplicity of small-town living, neighbors helping neighbors to get by, the respect a person earned from being decent and honest and hardworking. Those were the things that mattered to him now, the things he wanted in his life as badly as he wanted Dory and Jason.

Revealing his secrets and his hurts to her had brought a strange sense of calm to his turbulent soul. If only he could somehow instill that same feeling into his heart. Perhaps then the emotional walls would crumble and clear the way for him to love Dory in a way he had never loved a woman, fully, completely, with every fiber of his being. Until then, he continued to yearn to be a part of her life.

Only the impending court date gave him hope. If there had been any doubt in his mind before as to whether he could be a good father to Jason, there was none now. He suspected that Dory knew it, too.

He sensed her slow relinquishing of the hold she had on Jason, yielding a part of the boy over to him. Any day now, the courts would reach a decision. For the first time Ben felt confident that it would be favorable. But more than that, the unsealing of the adoption records would prove once and for all that what he had felt in his heart from the beginning was true, that he was Jason's father.

Yet sharing custody of Jason would constitute only a partial victory for him. He wanted more. Having had an intimate taste of Dory and the life she offered, he wanted it all.

Caught in the heat of Ben's stare, she felt herself weakening under it. She would have given herself to him right there, right then on the kitchen floor if he wanted it. She could feel the eagerness burning within her. Could he see it in her eyes? She didn't care.

She thought he was about to kiss her, and tilted her face up at him as her lashes swooped down over her eyes.

''Smells like something's burning,'' he said.

Dory's eyes snapped open like shutters on a windy day.

''The oven, Dory. Something's burning in the oven.''

In that instant she smelled it, too.

''The bread!'' she cried.

Grabbing an oven mitt from the counter, she raced to the stove and pulled open the door. Waves of smoke hit her in the face as she fumbled to get the pan out.

The bread smoked in the baking pan, crusty and burnt beyond recognition.

Dory laughed sheepishly. "I guess I wasn't paying attention."

"Let me give you a hand with that," he offered.

"There are plastic bags in the pantry. You can put it in one of those for now and I'll give it to the birds in the morning."

He was about to move, when the shrill sound of the smoke alarm startled him.

"Where's the circuit breaker?" he shouted above the noise.

"In the basement, next to the hot water heater. But—"

He ran from the room and downstairs to the place she said. Yanking the door open, he scanned the board. Nothing was marked. He began throwing switches, sending various parts of the house into darkness, and muttering an oath under his breath at his inability to find the right one. When every switch had been thrown and the sound still screeched from above, he raced back upstairs, taking the creaking basement steps two at a time.

At the doorway to the kitchen, he froze. There was Dory, standing on tiptoe on one of the kitchen chairs, arms raised above her head in an attempt to dismantle the smoke alarm. She worked swiftly and deftly to unwind the wires. Within seconds the screeching stopped and the room was plunged into the acute silence that comes in the wake of loud, protracted noise.

It reminded him of the silence that accompanied lights-out in prison, when the din of the day was suddenly hushed, and he was plunged into the awful dead quiet of the night.

Why did he have to think of something like that now? And then he realized it was because the person he'd been then, and the person he was now, were the same. Those terrible days helped make him the man he was today. And the woman standing tiptoe on the chair in the middle of the room helped him to live with it.

Dory looked down at him from her vantage point, and said, "I tried to tell you, but you ran out of here so fast."

"Does it always go off like that?"

"Only when I burn something in the oven."

He came to stand beside the chair and raised his arms to help her down. Her hands went to his shoulders for support as his fingers encircled her waist and he lifted her effortlessly to the floor.

"And that's the only way to fix it? You have to get up there?"

She shrugged with resignation.

"I'll have to do something about that," he said. "I'll get on it first thing in the morning."

"What are you going to do, rewire the whole house?" she teased.

"If I have to."

The possessiveness of his reply made her look at him curiously. "That would take some time to do, wouldn't it?"

He regretted instantly the impulsiveness of his reply. To imagine himself a part of all this was one thing. To say it out loud was quite another, especially when he had no reason to think that he would ever be.

"You're right," he replied instead. "In a couple of weeks it'll be Memorial Day and you won't be needing my help around here any longer. But I'd suggest you hire yourself a good electrician and get the place rewired."

The lighthearted atmosphere of just minutes ago vanished, and a sudden whiff of tension permeated the kitchen as strongly as the aroma of cooking food.

What he didn't say was that he might very well be around after Memorial Day. The fact was, he would be there until word arrived that their petition had been granted by the court. But even though the words remained unspoken, their shadow stretched over the room.

Dory turned her back to him and busied herself at the stove, stunned by the reality of their situation. They had made love and revealed their most painful, innermost secrets to each other, and still there remained the unresolved issue of Jason, like a chasm, dividing them right down the middle in spite of all her dreams to the contrary.

There was no ignoring the inevitable for either of them. As they waited for the decision from the court, the tension grew thicker and more palpable in spite of everything, and they both knew that whatever that decision was, their lives would be changed by it forever.

"Who are we kidding?" she heard him mutter across the room.

"You're right. This dinner was a stupid idea."

"That's not what I meant."

"I know what you meant." The dinner was a part of it, a part of the dream she had indulged in a moment of weakness, but she didn't say that to him. "You're right about that, too. Any way you cut it, the truth hurts."

He didn't like his meanings analyzed or second-guessed. How could she know what he was feeling, how deeply he longed for the kind of life she offered and how his own lack of belief stood in the way?

"What truth is that, Dory?" Something in his tone should have warned her that things were about to get more complicated.

"That you'll be leaving as soon as we hear from the court."

There, it was out. The words that hovered like phantoms all around them were finally spoken.

He smiled caustically into her eyes that were fixed defiantly upon him, as if daring him to refute it.

"Well, that's up to you, isn't it?"

Those beautiful green eyes looked at him petulantly. "You mean it's up to the court, don't you?"

"We both know in our hearts what the court is going to do. And when those adoption records are unsealed and we both learn the truth of what I've been telling you all along, we also both know that what happens after that will be up to you."

"I won't stand in your way if you want to petition the court for visitation rights. Is that what this is all about?"

His eyes were fixed tightly on her pale face. "I won't need your permission for that. That much *will* be up to the court."

"Then what are you talking about?" she demanded. The color rose to her cheeks as she grew more impatient and scared.

"I'm talking about courage, Dory. The courage to admit your feelings to someone else in spite of the consequences. The courage to admit the truth."

"I've never been afraid of the truth. No matter how much it hurts."

"Is that so? All right, so tell me how you feel about me."

"I think you're a good man. I think you're decent and honest, and—"

"I don't need a character reference, thank you. Besides, I didn't ask what you *think* of me. I want to know how you feel, I mean how you *really* feel, about me. Or if you have any feelings at all for me."

Dory stiffened at his ridicule. It would have been easy to toss off a caustic remark, to tell him how much she hated him for having turned her life upside down. Another person might have grasped the opportunity to wound him with indifference. But it was not in her nature to be cruel.

"Come on, Dory," he urged with angry impatience. "You're a smart woman, too smart not to know what I'm asking you."

He was backing her into a dangerous corner from which there was no escape.

"You want the truth?" she stormed at him. "All right. Yes! Yes, damn it, I have feelings for you. I...I... Oh God, I love you. I love you so much it frightens me."

She spoke each word as if she hated the sound of it, her features twisting with the bitter taste of the truth upon her tongue.

"All you have to do is look at me and I go weak all over. I've tried to fight it, but I can't. It's as if there's a part of me over which I have no control."

The words should have made him happy, but somehow, they didn't. She admitted her love to him as if it were the worst possible thing that could happen to her. What she said next stung him more deeply than he could have imagined.

"It was natural, I suppose, falling in love with you.

It's been such a long time for me, and I was feeling lonely and afraid, and I let you seduce me.''

Isn't that what he had done, let himself be seduced by her? Hearing her say it, however, sent his reason into a tailspin.

"I've never seduced any woman," he exclaimed. "I'm not interested in a woman who has to be coaxed. I want a woman who's willing and who's not afraid to show me what she wants, like I thought you were last night."

Dory cringed. Did he have to remind her of the way she had opened herself up to him, with the eagerness of a virgin all too willing to let herself be seduced?

"I want a woman who's not afraid to give back. Correct me if I'm wrong, but I had the distinct impression that that's what happened this afternoon. Or is that just how you show your gratitude?"

He knew his barb had hit its mark when her mouth fell open and he saw the sting of pain in her wide, green eyes.

His sarcasm was not lost on Dory as her mind spun with thoughts of the wanton, reckless passion she had exhibited, bringing it all back to her in a tidal wave of emotion.

"Gratitude?" she echoed. "Is that what you think it was? After I just admitted to what I feel for you?"

"Yeah, right, you love me. But you wish you didn't, because it just makes things more complicated. Because after we hear from the attorney, you'll go back to living your safe little life where you never have to tell any man that you love him ever again, and all you'll have to deal with is the pest who comes now and then to see his son."

"That's not fair," she exclaimed. "Do you think I can ever go back to the way things were before?"

"Then what are you going to do about it?"

"Wh-what do you mean?"

"Face it, Dory. This thing isn't going to go away, no matter how much you might want it to. You've admitted that you love me, the question remains, what are you going to do about it?"

She hated the smug, almost arrogant way in which he used her feelings against her. "Do? What makes you think I should do anything about it? You'll have what you want. You'll have your share of Jason."

"Is that all you think I want?"

"Isn't it? Tell me something, Ben. What will you do if you find out that you're not Jason's father?" She thought she already knew the answer to that. He would leave. Why would he stay when he had already proven that he didn't believe in love?

Ben's reaction to the bitter question was swift and genuine. "Not Jason's father? Sure I am. We both know that in our hearts, don't we?"

He had to be. He had long since given up the possibility that he wasn't.

"But what if you're not?"

It wasn't so much the words that cut him like a knife, it was the look on her face.

It was his turn to feel cornered. In a low, thick voice, he told her, "I've handled a lot worse and survived."

She shuddered to think of what he had endured in prison, and what he had lost. But it was no greater than the tragedies in her own life, and the one that threatened her now. To love him was the best and the worst thing that had ever happened to her. The best because it had helped dislodge the memories and ease the bite of their pain. The worst because she knew she would carry with her forever the burn of his lips against hers and the knowledge that he had never promised her forever.

His eyes flickered with dark emotion as they searched her face long and hard. He stood there without moving, wondering how he would ever survive this.

"Have it your way," he said. With a look of abject disappointment on his handsome face, he added haplessly, "Dinner's getting cold."

He was angry at her vulnerability—that he could hurt her as much as he did, and he was angry at himself for the desire that raged within him even now.

The color that flushed her face accentuated her delicate cheekbones. Her eyes blazed fury and indignation and hatred and love all at the same time, the green of them sparkling like emeralds in the candlelight. She was like a beautiful, angry cat with her back up, exciting him with her anger as acutely as she had excited him with her lovemaking.

His gaze was drawn to the rise and fall of her chest as her breathing came in rapid little bursts. Her breasts were thrust against the fabric of her blouse, the outline of her nipples straining toward him. He felt the strength of his desire, no longer a slow, steady surge of blood through his veins, but a rapid, heated arousal that pushed against his jeans.

She was in his head, in his blood, and it was suddenly no longer enough just to look at her. He wanted her with the same fierce desperation that had overtaken him last night. He could tell himself that what they felt for each other wasn't enough on which to build a life together, but it would never change the need he had established for her, or the passion that burned like a wildfire out of control.

Dory read his intentions in his eyes, which were fiery bright. She closed her own eyes against the impact. Pawn to her desire, she felt herself weakening under his hot, ardent gaze. Even now she felt her soft, private places heating up as if on fire, while her unanswered question about whether he would stay still hung in the air.

His eyes strayed to the table, and she knew what he was thinking. She could almost smell the pungent aroma of candles blown out in a hurry, and feel the crisp white lace beneath her back. With a soft intake of breath, she prepared herself to be taken in the rapid, angry rush of his desire.

She closed her eyes to the inevitable, fearing it, embracing it, wanting it more than she wanted life itself. From some far-off place she heard a noise. Her heartbeat? His? No, it didn't have the heavy, erratic sound of a heart beating out of control. She sought to ignore it as she waited for his lips to claim hers.

But the moment of possession never came.

Feeling him pull back, Dory opened her eyes and saw that something had distracted him.

She knew in an instant what it was. The sound she had heard was the telephone ringing.

Like an unwanted intruder it barged in, forcing its way between them, hurtling Dory from one kind of expectancy to another. Her first thought was that it was Martin calling and that something had happened.

She backed away from Ben, her eyes still locked to his, until she reached the doorway, and then she hurried out of the room to answer the phone.

The desk on which the telephone sat was no more than seconds away, but she was breathless nevertheless when she reached for it.

"Hello? What? Uh, yes, yes, this is she."

The voice at the other end of the line was not the one Dory had expected. Instead of her grandfather's anxious voice telling her of some mishap he and Jason had gotten into, a feminine voice answered back.

"This is Celina Bonham. I do hope I'm not interrupting anything."

Dory's entire being snapped to attention. "Why, Mrs. Bonham, no, you're not interrupting anything," she lied.

She turned a wild, stricken gaze toward the doorway. Ben was standing there, his whole body having gone rigid at the mention of the attorney's name. For a second he remained there, hands gripping the jambs for support as he struggled to suppress the passion that raged inside of him still. In several long strides he was at her side. Not asking her permission to listen in, he bent his dark head down toward hers and placed his ear to the phone.

Sharing the phone, they listened apprehensively, their heads bent together, practically cheek to cheek, their lips so close they could have kissed.

"I have good news for you," said the attorney.

Ben's heart slammed into his chest. Dory's skipped a beat with anticipation so acute it was like a physical thing.

"The court has approved your petition to open the file."

In a faraway voice that sounded stiff and vaguely like her own, Dory said, "That's wonderful."

Ben gave out with a triumphant whoop under his breath. "How soon can it be done?" he asked anxiously.

"Mr. Stone? Is that you?" The attorney sounded surprised to hear his voice on the line.

"How soon?" he repeated.

"Why, right now, if you like."

"You mean you have the file right there?" Dory asked, her panic growing.

"Yes. It was turned over to me late this afternoon. Would you like me to open it?"

Dory clamped her hand down hard over the mouthpiece and looked desperately at Ben. He looked as afraid and uncertain as she was. "Ben," she began, "whatever happens—"

He pulled her hand from the phone. Into the mouthpiece he commanded, "Open it."

They could hear the sound that the letter opener made as it slipped beneath the glued flap of the manila envelope that housed the file and ripped it open. They heard the sounds of papers being leafed through in rapid succession, as the searcher looked for one thing and one thing only. They could hear the sound of each other's heart beating a savage rhythm.

But they could not hear what was coming from the sound of the attorney's voice when, retaining her cool professionalism, she said, "The records, Mr. Stone, reflect that you are not the child's biological father."

Shock, at first. Cold, numbing shock.

Somewhere in the tumult of crushing disappointment Ben found his voice. In a voice ringing with desperation, he asked, "Are you certain?"

"Absolutely. It's right here. You understand, of

course, that I cannot reveal the actual biological father's name."

"Sure, sure." His mind was spinning out of control. Had Allison lied and put another man's name on the birth certificate to insure that he would never have his child? "The mother's name. Please, Mrs. Bonham, you have to tell me the mother's name."

"Mr. Stone, that's hardly possible. You agreed that—"

"To hell with what I agreed," he stormed. He was losing it, his control, his child, Dory, everything.

Dory's heart went out to him. He looked so utterly desperate. Placing her hand over his, she pulled the phone closer, giving him a warning look with her eyes not to interfere.

Her voice was level and softly pleading. "Mrs. Bonham, please. You see, it's possible that Mr. Stone's late wife might have lied about the father."

Ben's dark eyes widened and misted with a thousand unnamed emotions to hear Dory's gentle plea on his behalf.

She spoke in a whisper, as if hearing the words out loud might somehow make a mockery of the whole situation. "Please, Mrs. Bonham. This would mean so much to us."

There was nothing but static silence at the other end of the line at first, followed by a faintly resigning click of the tongue. "Oh, very well. But this is highly unusual."

Again, the shuffling of papers while the two of them waited with their hearts lodged in their throats.

"Let's see. Ah yes, here it is, the name of the mother."

There was a pause, only a fraction of a second really, but a lifetime to the two people who waited.

"I'm sorry, Mr. Stone, but the mother was not your late wife. It appears that the child in question is not yours."

Chapter 16

It was nothing but a coincidence, after all. A painful and poignant coincidence, but a coincidence nevertheless.

Everything became a blur after that. The phone fell out of his hand and he stumbled backward, the news hitting him with the impact of a fist in the solar plexus. He needed air. Somehow he made it to the front door.

He stood on the weathered planks of the porch, gulping in air the way a thirsty man gulps water. He found it hard to think. All he could do was feel. Desperation. Futility. Loss. No one word could describe the utter hopelessness he was feeling.

He didn't know how he came to be standing before the carousel, but it appeared suddenly in front of him, like a wall he had run smack up against. Stripped of its tarpaulins, its horses stood out like ghostly steeds, hooves thrashing against the night, bloodred nostrils flared, white teeth bared in taunting smiles. It was as if they were all laughing at him, at the weakness in him that had caused all this trouble and led to all this heartache.

He stood there staring wildly up at them, envying the lifelessness that freed them from the pain of feeling. Hating them for being a part of Dory and Jason's life when he would never be. "How?" he cried to them, as if they could hear him and somehow they alone knew the answer. "How could I have been so wrong?"

He thought his gut instincts had been sharpened in prison, honed to perfection by a life that made such things necessary for survival. What had happened to his instincts to make them so untrustworthy?

Was it love that made him disobey his intuitive voice and run contrary to his reason? Love, that made fools of everyone in one way or another?

Or was it need? Not the physical need he had for Dory. That was basic and fundamental, and he was just a man, with a man's hungers and needs, and he'd be damned if he would ever apologize for that. Rather, the obsessive need he had to find his son at any cost, the compulsive need to right the terrible wrong that had been done to him, and the desperate need to believe that Jason might be his.

But that was just it. Somewhere along the way he had lost sight of the *might be* and had created his own reality out of dreams. In those dreams he saw them all together, him, Dory, Jason and Martin, a happy, loving family, not just until Memorial Day, but for all the days after that. When all the while it was still just a fantasy never to come true.

My God, he thought, the torture he must have put

Dory through. Awash with guilt over the way he had hurt her, it did his conscience little good to know that she had fallen in love with him despite his threatening claim to her son and the dark secrets from his past that touched so deeply upon her own.

She had looked so scared that cool April morning when he had appeared on her doorstep. And so sad. She was that most lethal of things to a man, a beautiful and vulnerable woman. He knew now that he had lost his heart to her that day without even knowing it.

He should have been strong enough to confide his secret past early on and taken his chances. Maybe then things would never have gotten to this point. Maybe she would have sent him packing long before his suspicions had a chance to get a foothold in his mind and lead them to where they were now.

And where did that leave him? He still felt as desperate and alone as he had the day he arrived. He didn't have his son then, and he didn't have his son now. In the wake of the pain he had caused, there didn't seem to be anything left for him to do except leave the way he came, with his pack on his back. The only difference was that he would be carrying much more than his meager wardrobe with him. He would be carrying a hurt inside so fierce that it made all his previous hurts seem trivial in comparison.

He had survived those dark and lonely years in prison and endured the heartbreak of Allison's betrayal, but he didn't know if he could withstand the loss of Dory and Jason and everything he had come to believe in.

Just when he had come to accept his feelings for Dory, when he'd been about to grab a piece of happiness for himself as a part of her family, in the shattering aftermath of this evening's news, what was left for him there? After all, he bitterly reminded himself, Dory had never asked him to stay.

Why should she now that the threat had been removed? The look on her face tonight said it all. As they had stood there with their heads bent together toward the phone, her complexion had been ashen with anxiety, her beautiful features wrought with panic. When she had pleaded with the attorney to reveal the mother's name, even in the midst of his own turmoil, he'd been shocked to know that she did it for him.

Nevertheless, there had been no mistaking the wave of relief he saw wash over her face and the involuntary cry he heard spill from her lips when she heard the stunning news that Jason was not his. There could be little doubt about her feelings then.

He had gambled and he had lost, and the last thing his bruised and battered ego needed at the moment was Dory's pity. He turned his head and saw her standing there. Pulling in a deep, galvanizing breath, he said, "Congratulations, Dory, you won." He turned away, filled with self-disgust at the harshness he heard ringing in his tone.

There was no sign of pity in her voice or her eyes. "There's no victory here, Ben. Certainly not for me."

If only she knew what he was thinking, how badly he wanted her to want him, and how uncertain he was of being able to love her in return. Instead, he said, "I was thinking how your life can turn on a dime. God knows, mine has." He smothered a bitter little laugh. "I should be used to it, but I guess I never will be. What is it, my karma? Did I do something bad in a previous life?"

"Oh, Ben, surely you don't think that."

"Why not? Do you have a better explanation?"

"Yes, I do. It's called life."

"Are you telling me you don't believe in Karma?"

"I believe that there is an ultimate power by which the order of things is prescribed." She shrugged her shoulders as if to say, "go figure," and with a note of resignation in her voice, she concluded simply, "It's fate."

It was fate that led him to her doorstep one crisp April morning. Fate which decreed that their lives entwine the way they had. Fate had decided the outcome of their problem, and only fate would determine what was to become of them now.

"I can't blame it on anything but myself," he said dully.

"Don't you think you're being a little hard on yourself?"

"Think about it. I knew what I was getting into when I married Allison, but I married her anyway."

"You could never have known what she would do."

"Maybe not. But I was smart enough to know that she was marrying me for the kind of future I could give her. She came from a wealthy family and wasn't about to settle for anything less."

"It was a mistake, Ben. That's all. Just a mistake. We all make them. I've certainly made my share. Look at the person I married. I've been carrying the burden of that particular mistake around with me every day for the past three years. But you taught me something. You taught me that there comes a time when you have to let go and get on with your life."

He turned sharply to look at her. In the moonlight

her expression was all calm and reason. It made him angry to see it, when his own calm had fled long ago and his reason was spinning out of control.

"How did I teach you that?" he scoffed. "All I did was sit there."

"But don't you see? It was enough for me to know that somebody cared enough to sit there and listen."

"Somebody?" he questioned.

"You. All right? You."

"Look, Dory, I don't blame you for any of this. You didn't ask for me to come barging into your life and turn it upside down the way I did. Not only didn't you ask for it, but you don't deserve it. You have enough baggage of your own to handle. You don't deserve what I put you through because of the baggage I carry around with me. All I'm saying is that I take full responsibility for my actions."

"How noble of you."

His dark eyes flared at the undisguised sarcasm in her tone.

"Don't look at me like that," she told him. "If you expect me to feel sorry for you because you think it's all your fault, you can forget it. Besides, it sounds to me like you're feeling sorry enough for yourself."

Her insensitivity to his feelings shocked him. It was so unlike her. And then he realized what she was doing. She was a clever one, all right, accusing him of self-pity and forcing him to take a good, hard look at himself. And he didn't like what he saw.

Never once during those torturous years in prison had he ever felt sorry for himself. If anything, the experience had hardened his resolve to remain strong. Yet here he was, indulging in self-pity and hating himself for it. Until Dory had the courage to speak out and make him see it for what it was.

He turned away, disgusted with himself. "You're right. It wasn't self-pity that got me through those bad times, and it won't be self-pity that will get me through this one."

"What will you do?" she asked.

He shrugged his broad shoulders helplessly and answered, "Move on, I guess. See what's around the next turn in the road."

It wasn't what Dory had expected him to say. Unprepared for his response, she felt as if the rug had been pulled out from under her. She quickly regained her equilibrium and said, "I meant about your son. Will you continue to search for him?"

"I'm no longer sure I'm meant to find him," he replied fatalistically.

"So, you'll be leaving, then?" She was thunderstruck, trying hard to comprehend what his leaving would do to her. Her voice emerged as a scratchy whisper. "When?"

"In the morning."

The words stung like a slap across the cheek. "So soon?"

He gestured toward the carousel and said, "You seem to have everything under control now. The rest of the floor needs sanding and buffing, but I've patched that hole in the roof as best I can. There's no reason why you can't open on Memorial Day as planned."

"Planned?" She spoke the word dully as she turned away to hide her tears. "Yes, that's what I had planned, wasn't it?"

How could she have known weeks ago, when her

goal had been simply to make it to Memorial Day, how it would change to include all the Memorial Days yet to come, with this man beside her? Yes, with a few finishing touches, she would be ready to open on Memorial Day, but without Ben there, it wouldn't be the same.

She had come out there to tell him that, to tell him how very much she loved him and to ask him to stay. But what was the point, when he seemed to have made up his mind to leave, choosing the open road over her, choosing a child he would never know to the son that she wanted more than anything to share with him.

Dory was stunned by the apparent ease with which he could just walk away. But it was more than her own crushed feelings she was thinking about. What effect would Ben's leaving have on Jason? He had been too young to feel the effect of Eddie's absence, but this was different. Ben had become as much a part of their lives as any real father ever could be. Jason looked up to him. His time spent with Ben building the model airplane was all he talked about. She recalled with tears in her eyes that just that very morning he had said to her, "Mommy, I wanna be just like Ben when I grow up."

Children were resilient, she told herself. In time, his broken little heart would mend, and although he would always feel the absence of a father in his life, in time, the memory of the man who had spent this spring with them would fade.

For herself, however, it was different. It was funny, but she had known Ben only a few weeks, yet it felt as if she'd known him and loved him all her life. With cold certainty, she knew she would carry the pain of his leaving with her for a very long time.

All the energy flowed out of her, and suddenly she felt overwhelmingly tired. The weeks of waiting for the court's decision had taken their toll. What she had once looked upon with dread had come to take on a different meaning these last few days when she had begun to feel the stirrings of hope from deep within. She stood there, not knowing what to do or say, her unhappiness mirrored in the teardrops that slipped silently down her cheeks, glistening in the starlight from above. The feel of her heart breaking into a million pieces was unbearable. That she found her voice in the midst of her gloom was a miracle. That the words that emerged were a brave attempt to hide her sorrow was the saddest thing of all.

"There's no need to tell Martin about it. I'll simply tell him in the morning that you had to leave. I'll say that you had previous commitments...other priorities. He'll understand."

"And Jason?" he asked, his tone echoing his deep concern.

Leaving Dory was torture enough, but leaving Jason only made the heartache worse. Jason had become a bright spot in his life. He had come to look forward to their hour together each night after Jason's bath. The little guy was a fast learner. He only had to be shown something once to know how to do it when asked. He could just picture the model airplanes that would hang in Jason's room when he was old enough to build them by himself. Maybe one of them would even be the P-51 Mustang bomber they'd worked on together.

"Jason has his whole life to get over it," said Dory. She spoke at the ground, her eyes averted, so he would not see her tears.

His face was shadowed by guilt. "You don't think he'll have nightmares or anything, do you? Remember that night he woke up crying that there were monsters under his bed?"

She remembered. She had heard Jason cry out in the middle of the night and had jumped out of bed and hurried to his room. Ben was already there. Checking in the closet and under the bed and finding no monsters, he had soothed Jason back to sleep while Dory had watched speechless and grateful.

"Monsters are real to Jason," she said. "He sees them on television, in books. But something like this, it doesn't have a scary face or a terrible roar. Don't get me wrong. He feels it. Children are amazingly adept at sensing things. But if he can't attach an ugly face to it, in a way, it's not real."

"So what you're saying is that Jason will be just fine."

Dory knew there were no guarantees in life. Nevertheless, she echoed, "Just fine."

And neither of them believed it.

"If you want, I can make you some breakfast before you go."

Her kindness was too much for him to bear. "Yeah, that would be great," he mumbled, knowing in his heart that he would be gone before then.

She turned to go.

"Dory?"

The appeal in his voice was low and slightly unsteady, but audible. The sound of her name softly uttered halted her in her tracks and turned her slowly back around.

A moment of taut silence followed.

He flashed her a smile that was so genuine and so beautiful that it took her breath away.

"Thanks," he said. "For everything."

Later, as he stood at the bedroom window for what was to be the last time, he reflected on how much he had meant what he said. He couldn't hate, not when he had so much to thank her for. She had given him a job when he needed one badly. She had invited him into her home without question or suspicion. She had provided him with an opportunity to relate to a child for the first time in his life. She had been honest and fair with him about Jason in spite of what she stood to lose. She had filled his physical need in ways he had not thought possible. But most of all, she had come to love him in spite of his past mistakes.

He thought of all the people who, in their entire lifetimes, would never experience the kind of passion he had found with Dory. He himself would never have known that it existed had it not been for one brave and incredibly sexy woman. He should have been happy to have known that kind of passion at all, to have been even the smallest part of her life. Yet there remained inside of him an empty, aching place that only she could fill.

There was no telling where his path would lead him. Only one thing was certain. No matter which road he followed, it would take him farther away from everything he couldn't have—the wife, the kid, the happiness and security of family life.

He turned from the window and went to the dresser. From the top drawer he removed the few pieces of clothes that were neatly folded there and laid them on the bed. At the closet he pulled his worn denim shirt from the hanger and put it on in place of the newer one he had put on earlier for dinner.

He had to laugh at how nervous he had been wondering whether or not she would notice that he was wearing his good pair of jeans and the new shirt he had purchased on a recent trip into town. One look at her, though, and his nervousness flew right out the window.

She had looked so beautiful dressed in a white silk blouse with a flounce of ruffles at the dipping neckline and a skirt that brushed the tops of her knees. He had never seen her wearing either before. His heart had done a little somersault knowing that she had dressed especially for dinner and that, from the soft blush on her face, she was just as nervous as he was about it.

He pulled his backpack down from the top shelf in the closet and tossed it onto the bed. Absently, he shoved his clothes into it, not caring if they got wrinkled. He'd worry about that some other time.

He slipped into his brown leather flight jacket and hoisted the pack onto his back. On his way to the door he grabbed his watch from the dresser.

Funny how time had lost all meaning to him in this place. Here, the hours were marked by events rather than the hands of a clock. Breakfast was at seven. At eight Jason left for preschool. By two he was home. Dinner was at six. Jason's bath time was at seven. From seven-thirty until eight-thirty he and Jason built the plane together. At eight-thirty it was story time and then lights out for Jason. At nine he would invariably find Martin outside on the porch, sitting in his rocking chair and smoking his pipe. By nine-thirty, with her chores for the day finished, Dory would join them for an hour or so of quiet conversation. By eleven he'd be up in his room, standing at the window, waiting for the light to come on in the carousel. When it did, he would watch for a while and then go to bed, only to get up in the morning and repeat the whole thing over again. No, there was no need to tell time when he had the simple, pleasurable events of the day to go by.

With a ragged sigh, he strapped the watch to his wrist. He took a step toward the door, but stopped.

His footsteps took him back to the window where the Catskill mountains in the distance looked like great rolling shadows against the darkness. His heart sank when he didn't see the reassuring light in the carousel.

It was well past midnight when Ben left the room and made his way noiselessly down the hall. He stopped in front of Jason's door, wondering whether or not to wake him up to say goodbye, and deciding that there was no sense trying to explain it to a four-year-old, nor in compounding his own pain. But he couldn't resist peeking in at the boy as he slept. Then, with a full heart, he left the room, and all that he'd once dreamed of.

Downstairs he could smell the remains of their uneaten French dinner as he passed the kitchen. Hardening himself against the onrush of emotion it brought, he hurried on toward the front door.

The screen door creaked on its hinges when he opened it and stepped outside.

A crescent moon hung low in the sky, like a jagged tear in the black cloth of night. With no surrounding lights to obscure them, a million stars winked back at him. There was comfort in knowing that they would always be up there. At this point, they were the only constant in his life.

He scanned the midnight sky, searching out the ones

he recognized like old friends. There was Orion, the Hunter. He had pointed him out to Jason one night from the front porch, and for days after Jason had proudly told everyone how he had seen O'Brien in the sky.

Was there nothing he could think about that would not remind him of Jason? Was there nowhere he could turn that he did not see Dory's haunting and beautiful face before him?

For years he had felt something missing from his life. He had been foolish enough to think that marrying Allison would satisfy his longing not only to love but to be loved back. Not for his money or his position, but for himself. But, of course, it hadn't. The ache remained, reaching into the deepest corners of his heart.

It wasn't until he met a beautiful woman with sad green eyes that the ache began to subside. With Dory he had come as close as he would ever get to fulfilling the need that raged inside of him. But the joke was on him. To come that close, only to be left with the same aching need.

The pain of losing her was almost physical, and yet he embraced it, for at least it meant that he was alive and not the half-dead man he had been before knowing her. Like her namesake, she had unleashed sorrow and misery, if not upon all mankind, then surely upon him. But she had also given him the one thing that was left inside the box. She had given him hope.

It was astonishing to him that he could feel anything at all except the pain and misery of losing her, yet there it was, beating faintly within him, the tiniest bit of hope that he would one day get over her.

He looked around. This was where it all began. This

was where he had first seen her. She'd had grease on her face and a wrench in her hand, and he had thought her crazy for thinking that she could get the Dutch Mill in shape by Memorial Day.

She had looked so scared that cool April morning when he had appeared on her doorstep. And so sad. She was that most lethal of things, a beautiful and vulnerable woman. He knew now that he had lost his heart to her that day without even knowing it.

He wasn't shocked to discover that he loved her. Hadn't he somehow known that very first day? What he felt instead was an overwhelming sense of relief that he was finally able to acknowledge it, if not to Dory, then at least to himself.

Yet with the knowledge came an indescribable sadness to be leaving behind him all that he had come to hold dear. Well, at least, they had accomplished the seemingly impossible task of getting the Dutch Mill ready to open on Memorial Day.

The big horse they brought back from Devil's Corner needed work, but the roof was patched, and it wasn't likely that anyone would notice that there were some finishing touches to be made to some of the horses.

Together, they had gotten the job done. And as he stood with his feet braced atop the weathered planks, the midnight breeze rustling the hair at his forehead, one word kept repeating over and over in Ben's mind.

Together.

Wasn't that the way they were supposed to be? The three of them? Together?

Chapter 17

She couldn't bring herself to work on the carousel. Not even her old friends could assuage the terrible pain of Ben's leaving.

Instead, she lay awake in bed with the covers thrown back, feeling feverish despite the cool night breeze that billowed the curtains at the open window, trying hard to comprehend why he was leaving when so much had happened between them.

Perhaps he didn't feel the same way about love as she did. To her, love was more than the fulfillment of sexual desire. It was all encompassing. It was forever. You didn't walk away from it at the first sign of trouble.

She thought she had loved Eddie. That's why she had stayed. But she realized now that she never really loved him. He had represented something familiar to her, and it was that which she loved. Sadly, he had turned into a stranger at the end. It seemed that Ben wasn't the only one guilty of marrying for the wrong reasons.

Her feelings for Ben, on the other hand, were different. There were the cozy, warm feelings that came after they made love, when he was holding her in his arms and their breathing came in unison, as if they were one entity. There were the uncertain feelings, the ones that sprang from fear of the unknown, from loving blindly and not knowing where it would lead. There was the feeling of joy that came from being loved in return. The incredible physical pleasure of being with a man whose body fit so perfectly with hers. The feeling of unfamiliarity, of not knowing very much about him, and the resulting sense of excitement that came from being with a stranger. There were the tender feelings that ultimately arose when his past was revealed and she understood at last the cause of the pain she'd always seen in his eyes.

But most of all, there was the feeling of being caught in a wildfire out of control.

There was no denying the desire that raged between them, but that was just it. Men were creatures of the flesh, and maybe all they ever felt for women was really just animal desire. Was that why Ben was able to walk away? All right then, even though she would never understand it, apparently he could walk away from her and everything she had to offer in favor of…what had he called it? The next turn in the road. But that left one glaring question unanswered. How could he walk away from Jason? How many turns in the road would he have to come to before realizing that he would never find his son? That his search was worse than looking for a needle in a haystack?

She had lied to him tonight when she told him that

Jason would be just fine. She had done that for his sake. He seemed to be genuinely concerned for Jason's welfare, and she hadn't wanted to make things worse by telling him the truth.

He wouldn't be around to see Jason's tears. He wouldn't have to suffer through the pitiful questions of a four-year-old who was too young to understand. But she would. She could just hear him asking between sobs, "But why, Mommy? Why did Ben leave? Isn't he ever coming back?"

She thought he had come to love Jason. Could she have been mistaken? Could it have been just kindly tolerance that he had exhibited toward her son? Or had it been her imagination playing tricks on her, knowing how much she had wanted it to be so?

She tossed and turned, plagued by questions to which she had no answers. Just when she had learned to put her fears aside, when the risk of not getting involved had become greater than the risk of romantic involvement, he was leaving. He was wrong when he told her once that in the face of every misfortune there was always hope. Where was her hope now?

She must have dozed off, exhausted by her misery, only to awaken sometime later to the sound of the rusty hinges on the screen door. She knew that he would not wait until morning, that she had cooked him his last breakfast, had seen his handsome face for the last time. She flung herself onto her stomach and wept inconsolably into her pillow, knowing that he was gone, taking with him not only her heart, but her hope.

Dawn was breaking over the treetops when she opened her eyes. Despite her exhaustion from a night tortured with thoughts and dreams of Ben, Dory pulled herself out of bed. Dressed in the T-shirt in which she had slept, she left her room.

At the end of the hallway, she paused in front of the door to Ben's room. Shoring up her defenses, she grasped the knob with trembling fingers and opened it. The room was empty, the bed neatly made. The only hint of him was the faint masculine aroma in the air.

A rush of emotion hit her like a strong winter wind. She closed the door quickly and hurried toward the stairs. Jason would be up soon with a million questions that she would be unable to avoid. And she wasn't certain she could take the look in her grandfather's eyes just yet. For now, feeling the profound and sudden loss of Ben, she was grateful for the solitude of early morning in which to regroup.

But the smell of bacon frying in the pan as she descended the stairs erased any hope of time to herself before beginning this difficult day. Martin was up, she thought with a groan. She rolled her eyes at the thought of having to explain it all to him. Oh well, it was now or never. Gearing herself up for his reaction and the look of disappointment that was bound to appear in his eyes, she took a deep breath and walked into the kitchen.

"Hey, sleepyhead. I was beginning to think it would take a dousing with cold water to rouse you."

Dory froze in the doorway. That wasn't her grandfather's thin voice that greeted her, as she had expected, but a deep, melodious timbre that sent chills down her spine. It wasn't Martin standing with his back to her at the stove, but a tall, muscular form that made her throat go dry. It wasn't her grandfather's kindly, seamed face that turned to look at her, but the

handsome face she had carried with her into her
dreams last night, the one she thought she would never
see again.

Was she dreaming? Was it really him? She thought
she'd heard him leave in the dead of night. Her voice
was part whisper, part plea.

"Ben?" The sight of him brought a sense of profound relief, yet she questioned, "Wh-what are you
doing?"

From over a broad shoulder he flashed her a daz-
zling smile that threatened the remaining threads of
her self-control. "You said you were going to make
me breakfast, remember? But when you weren't up, I
figured I'd do it myself."

"Oh." The air went out of her like a burst balloon.
"Yes, I remember. I'm sorry. I didn't think... That is,
I thought... Here, let me do that." She came hesitantly
forward.

Barely reaching his shoulder in her bare feet, she
felt small and fragile beside him. She reached for the
fork he was holding, and the brush of his fingers
against hers sent a volt of electricity through her as if
she had put her finger in a socket.

She pulled her hand away quickly, the color rising
to her cheeks, and with the fork she poked at the strips
of bacon in the pan. The fat sputtered and hissed.
Without warning a burst of hot fat splattered against
the back of her hand. With a cry of pain, she dropped
the fork.

"Let me see that." Without waiting for her approval, he grasped her small white hand in his big one
to examine it. "That looks nasty," he concluded.

"It's n-nothing," she managed.

"Nonsense. It's blistering already. Come over here."

He led her to the sink where he gave the tap a quick twist and held her hand beneath a numbing stream of cold water. "Do you have anything in the medicine chest for this?"

His touch was more lethal to her than any burn from bacon grease. Unnerved by the sensations it caused, she replied, "I keep some aloe vera gel in the refrigerator."

With rapid strides across the hardwood floor, he went to the refrigerator and returned with a jar of clear gel that he scooped up onto the tips of his fingers and applied ever so gently to her burned skin.

The cold gel worked quickly to relieve the sting. Now, if there was only some way to ease the terrible burning inside.

"Thank you," she said. "It feels much better." Withdrawing her hand from his, she bent to retrieve the fork from the floor and then reached for a sponge to wipe up the grease that had splattered over the stove.

He watched her as she cleaned up the grease and then busied herself with fixing the rest of his breakfast. With her unbrushed hair strewn wildly about her face and shoulders, dressed only in a T-shirt that reached to just above her knees, smelling sweet and warm with sleep, she was the sexiest thing Ben had ever seen. His desire for her was as great and as quick as it ever was.

She knew he was watching her. Trying to remain calm, she said, "I didn't expect to see you here this morning."

"To tell you the truth, neither did I."

"Then why are you here?"

Smiling at her directness, he said mischievously, "The breakfast excuse won't do?"

She tossed him a sour look.

"I didn't think so."

He came to stand beside her, dangerously close but not touching. "I spent all night thinking about how I would say this. But seeing you this morning doesn't make it any easier."

"Look, Ben, there's no need to explain. I understand."

"Really? Then maybe you can explain it to me, Dory, because I don't."

"It's easy enough to understand. You care for Jason, but since he's not the son you wanted, you might as well be moving on."

"If only that were true," he said. "It would make walking away so much easier."

"What do you want from me?" she asked. Her eyes searched his hard for understanding. "Do you want me to help you make it easier to leave?"

"No, Dory. I want you to make it harder. I want you to make it impossible."

"How can I do that when you already know how I feel?"

She turned away, but he reached for her unexpectedly, his hand clamping down hard over her forearm to force her back around. Despite the panicky look on her face, he said, "Right. You love me. But you'll excuse me if I have a hard time accepting that when it was spoken in anger. That was how you said it, wasn't it?"

She thought back to the argument they'd had last night while the coq au vin had sat there getting cold.

"I...yes, I was angry. But I meant what I said. You're the one who seems to have a hard time with the truth."

He released her from his grip. "What is that supposed to mean?"

"I asked you last night what you would do if Jason was not your son. You still haven't answered the question."

Still expecting that he planned to leave, she was surprised by the response she received.

He began to laugh. It wasn't the kind of laughter that comes from having heard something genuinely funny, but rather from the relief of finally understanding what this was all about.

He reached for her this time with both hands, grasping her by the shoulders, fingers biting into her tender flesh as he pulled her toward him.

"Don't you know that I love you?"

There, it was out, and the release that came with the simple utterance brought with it a freedom he hadn't even felt the day he walked out of prison. It suddenly seemed like the most natural thing in the world to tell her how much she meant to him, and yet his heart hammered like a schoolboy's in his chest.

"I love you so much that at times I feel like I'm going to explode. I love the aching vulnerability that I see in your eyes. I love the passion that burns naked and raw inside of you. I love *you*, Dory. I would love you anytime, anywhere. Do I love you knowing that I'm not Jason's father? Even more, if such a thing is possible. Don't you see? That news last night freed me to love you with no strings attached."

"But you're leaving," she blurted out, pushing him away to arm's length.

"Only if you want me to."

"What about your son? He's out there, somewhere. Don't you want to find him?"

"I realized something else last night, Dory. This is where I belong. Right here at the Dutch Mill with you and Jason and Martin. Not wandering some aimless path in search of a dream that doesn't exist. And what if I ever do find my son? Do you think I could take him away from the people who love him? Besides, I could never love him more than I love Jason."

He dropped his arms from her shoulders and took a step back. Softly, he admitted, "I was all set to leave. Packed and everything. But something stopped me. One word brought me back. One word that describes the way it was meant to be. Together, Dory. We were meant to be together."

With a cry of joy she melted against him. "I was so afraid you didn't want us."

"Not want you?" he echoed incredulously, as if the sheer impossibility of the words rendered them meaningless to him. "God, Dory, you and Jason are *all* I want."

This time the tears that wet his shirt were tears of happiness. "When I thought I had lost you, I didn't know what to do," she said.

With the tip of his finger beneath her chin, he lifted her face to his and kissed her lightly on the lips. "Do you want me to stay?"

"Oh, yes," she breathed against his mouth. "More than anything."

He broke away slightly to look at her and venture, "How long did you have in mind?"

Dory's lashes swooped down to hide her eyes. Shyly, she answered, "I was thinking of forever."

In a warm rush of breath at her ear, he said, "You

realize what forever means, don't you? It means you'll have to marry me.''

Dory leaned pliantly against him, her heart racing in time with his. She felt secure in his arms, protected by his strength. But most of all she felt the overwhelming power of his love.

''Yes,'' she whispered, ''I'll marry you. On one condition.''

He hugged her tighter, promising, ''Anything.''

''I would like you to formally adopt Jason.''

Ben's joy was now complete. It was the fulfillment of the thing he had dreamed of all his life. Her love covered him like a pair of angel wings, drawing him snugly into the fold of her family. At last he was a part of something.

He could scarcely contain the emotion that welled up inside of him as he took her hand in his and said, his eyes shining with love, ''Come on. Let's go wake up Jason and tell him the news.''

Epilogue

Memorial Day broke bright and sunny. From miles around crowds flocked to the Dutch Mill. The cotton candy machine merrily spun its sugary confection. The games of chance lured the foolhardy to try their luck. The petting zoo brought squeals of delight from the little ones.

The lilting calliope music of the carousel drifted on currents of warm spring air all up and down the Delaware Valley. With the horses restored to their original ornate condition, and the gilded roof fixed as good as new, no one would ever have guessed how close it had all come to ruin.

Happily spinning cotton candy, Dory couldn't remember a time when the place had been so alive with fun and excitement, but most of all so filled with love.

Her eyes scanned the surroundings. Amid the happy, smiling faces of her neighbors, she saw Martin, pitching the brightly painted games like a carnival pro.

Jason sat astride the big black stallion with the red martingale, reaching frantically with his little arm in an attempt to claim the brass ring.

"Daddy, look how far I can reach!"

From where he stood at the controls to the carousel, Ben waved his hand.

It was hard to believe that Jason was almost six years old now, and that a whole year had gone by since that morning they had awakened him to tell him that they were getting married.

He had rubbed the sleep from his eyes and looked up at them with the most precious expression on his face and asked shyly, "Does that mean that Ben will be my daddy?"

The word that had thrilled Ben when he heard it for the first time that morning one year ago, reverberated throughout his entire being with the same excitement and pride at hearing it now.

Surrounded by the rhythmic prance of the painted ponies, Ben's heart was filled with contentment and joy. He had found peace at last. But more than that he had found a love so strong he shuddered from its impact.

He felt like old Rip van Winkle himself, having awakened from a long, deathlike sleep among the dark cloves of the mountaintop and come to this peaceful green valley surrounded by the softly rolling Catskills. Dory had told him once that from here you could see all creation, and she'd been right. All he had to do was look around him now to see all the creation that mattered.

His eyes searched eagerly between the passing horses for a sign of his wife. He spotted her chatting with one of the women from the nearby town while she spun a cotton candy cone for one of the children. She looked so radiantly happy running her precious Dutch Mill, surrounded by all the warm and familiar things she loved so much.

Their eyes met across the distance and held each other's gaze for many long moments when there was no need for words, only the love that raced back and forth between them.

The sadness was gone from her beautiful green eyes, replaced by a sparkle so bright that it rivaled the sunshine of this perfect spring day. The melancholy was absent from her soft-toned voice, chased away by. the warm, throaty laughter that came so easily these days.

With a smile that never failed to thrill him, she turned back to her work. He saw the neighbor point to her belly, and watched as Dory acknowledged the gesture by placing both hands lovingly against her softly swelling flesh.

A feeling of unbounding joy and pride overwhelmed him at the sight of her swollen profile. Deep within her was the child they had made together out of love. A little sister or brother for Jason. Another grandchild for Martin. And, at long last, a child of his own.

*   *   *   *   *

Take 4 bestselling love stories FREE

Plus get a FREE surprise gift!

Special Limited-time Offer

Mail to Silhouette Reader Service™

3010 Walden Avenue
P.O. Box 1867
Buffalo, N.Y. 14240-1867

YES! Please send me 4 free Silhouette Intimate Moments® novels and my free surprise gift. Then send me 6 brand-new novels every month, which I will receive months before they appear in bookstores. Bill me at the low price of $3.34 each plus 25¢ delivery and applicable sales tax, if any.* That's the complete price and a savings of over 10% off the cover prices—quite a bargain! I understand that accepting the books and gift places me under no obligation ever to buy any books. I can always return a shipment and cancel at any time. Even if I never buy another book from Silhouette, the 4 free books and the surprise gift are mine to keep forever.

245 BPA A3UW

Name	(PLEASE PRINT)	
Address	Apt. No.	
City	State	Zip

This offer is limited to one order per household and not valid to present Silhouette Intimate Moments® subscribers. *Terms and prices are subject to change without notice. Sales tax applicable in N.Y.

UMOM-698

©1990 Harlequin Enterprises Limited

At last the wait is over...
In March
New York Times bestselling author

NORA ROBERTS

will bring us the latest from the Stanislaskis as
Natasha's now very grown-up stepdaughter,
Freddie, and Rachel's very sexy brother-in-law
Nick discover that love is worth waiting for in

WAITING FOR NICK
Silhouette Special Edition #1088

and in April
visit Natasha and Rachel again—or meet them
for the first time—in

The Stanislaski Sisters

containing TAMING NATASHA
and FALLING FOR RACHEL

Available wherever Silhouette books are sold.

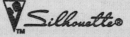

Look us up on-line at:http://www.romance.net   NRSS

As seen on TV!
Free Gift Offer

With a Free Gift proof-of-purchase from any Silhouette® book,
you can receive a beautiful cubic zirconia pendant.

This gorgeous marquise-shaped stone is a genuine cubic
zirconia—accented by an 18" gold tone necklace.

(Approximate retail value $19.95)

Send for yours today...

compliments of ▼ *Silhouette*®

To receive your free gift, a cubic zirconia pendant, send us one original proof-of-
purchase, photocopies not accepted, from the back of any Silhouette Romance™,
Silhouette Desire®, Silhouette Special Edition®, Silhouette Intimate Moments®
or Silhouette Yours Truly™ title available in February, March and April at your favorite
retail outlet, together with the Free Gift Certificate, plus a check or money order for
$1.65 U.S./$2.15 CAN. (do not send cash) to cover postage and handling, payable
to Silhouette Free Gift Offer. We will send you the specified gift. Allow 6 to 8 weeks for
delivery. Offer good until April 30, 1997 or while quantities last. Offer valid in the
U.S. and Canada only.

Free Gift Certificate

Name: _____

Address: _____

City: _____ State/Province: _____ Zip/Postal Code: _____

Mail this certificate, one proof-of-purchase and a check or money order for postage
and handling to: SILHOUETTE FREE GIFT OFFER 1997. In the U.S.: 3010 Walden
Avenue, P.O. Box 9077, Buffalo NY 14269-9077. In Canada: P.O. Box 613, Fort Erie,
Ontario L2Z 5X3.

FREE GIFT OFFER   084-KFD
ONE PROOF-OF-PURCHASE
To collect your fabulous FREE GIFT, a cubic zirconia pendant, you must include this
original proof-of-purchase for each gift with the properly completed Free Gift Certificate.

084-KFD

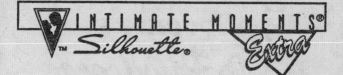

INTIMATE MOMENTS®
Silhouette® Extra

For an *EXTRA*-special treat, pick up

THE PERFECT COUPLE
by
Maura Seger

In April of 1997, Intimate Moments proudly features Maura Seger's *The Perfect Couple*, #775.

Everyone always said that Shane Dutton and Brenna O'Hare were the perfect couple. But they weren't convinced...not until a plane crash separated them, leaving Brenna at home to agonize and Shane to fight for his life in the frigid Alaskan tundra. Suddenly they began to realize just how perfect for each other they were. And they prayed...for a second chance.

In future months, look for titles with the EXTRA flash for more excitement, more romance—simply *more....*

INTIMATE MOMENTS®
Silhouette®

SHERRYL WOODS

32989	BEACH LANE	___	$7.99 U.S.	___	$9.99 CAN.
32979	MOONLIGHT COVE	___	$7.99 U.S.	___	$9.99 CAN.
32977	ASK ANYONE	___	$7.99 U.S.	___	$9.99 CAN.
32976	ALONG CAME TROUBLE	___	$7.99 U.S.	___	$9.99 CAN.
32975	ABOUT THAT MAN	___	$7.99 U.S.	___	$9.99 CAN.
32962	WELCOME TO SERENITY	___	$7.99 U.S.	___	$9.99 CAN.
32961	SEAVIEW INN	___	$7.99 U.S.	___	$9.99 CAN.
32947	DRIFTWOOD COTTAGE	___	$7.99 U.S.	___	$9.99 CAN.
32927	THE BACKUP PLAN	___	$7.99 U.S.	___	$9.99 CAN.
32893	FEELS LIKE FAMILY	___	$7.99 U.S.	___	$9.99 CAN.
32887	STEALING HOME	___	$7.99 U.S.	___	$9.99 CAN.
32852	A CHESAPEAKE SHORES CHRISTMAS	___	$16.95 U.S.	___	$19.95 CAN.
32846	HONEYSUCKLE SUMMER	___	$7.99 U.S.	___	$9.99 CAN.
32845	SWEET TEA AT SUNRISE	___	$7.99 U.S.	___	$9.99 CAN.
32814	RETURN TO ROSE COTTAGE	___	$7.99 U.S.	___	$9.99 CAN.
32756	HOME IN CAROLINA	___	$7.99 U.S.	___	$9.99 CAN.
32753	AMAZING GRACIE	___	$7.99 U.S.	___	$9.99 CAN.
32751	HOME AT ROSE COTTAGE	___	$7.99 U.S.	___	$9.99 CAN.
32641	HARBOR LIGHTS	___	$7.99 U.S.	___	$8.99 CAN.
32634	FLOWERS ON MAIN	___	$7.99 U.S.	___	$8.99 CAN.
32626	THE INN AT EAGLE POINT	___	$7.99 U.S.	___	$7.99 CAN.
31289	A SLICE OF HEAVEN	___	$7.99 U.S.	___	$9.99 CAN.
31288	FLIRTING WITH DISASTER	___	$7.99 U.S.	___	$9.99 CAN.

(limited quantities available)

TOTAL AMOUNT	$	_____
POSTAGE & HANDLING	$	_____
($1.00 for 1 book, 50¢ for each additional)		
APPLICABLE TAXES*	$	_____
TOTAL PAYABLE	$	_____

(check or money order—please do not send cash)

To order, complete this form and send it, along with a check or money order for the total above, payable to MIRA Books, to: **In the U.S.:** 3010 Walden Avenue, P.O. Box 9077, Buffalo, NY 14269-9077; **In Canada:** P.O. Box 636, Fort Erie, Ontario, L2A 5X3.

Name: _____
Address: _____ City: _____
State/Prov.: _____ Zip/Postal Code: _____
Account Number (if applicable): _____
075 CSAS

*New York residents remit applicable sales taxes.
*Canadian residents remit applicable GST and provincial taxes.

HARLEQUIN®
www.Harlequin.com

MSW0811BL

REQUEST YOUR FREE BOOKS!

2 FREE NOVELS
FROM THE ROMANCE COLLECTION
PLUS 2 FREE GIFTS!

YES! Please send me 2 FREE novels from the Romance Collection and my 2 FREE gifts (gifts are worth about $10). After receiving them, if I don't wish to receive any more books, I can return the shipping statement marked "cancel." If I don't cancel, I will receive 4 brand-new novels every month and be billed just $5.99 per book in the U.S. or $6.49 per book in Canada. That's a saving of at least 25% off the cover price. It's quite a bargain! Shipping and handling is just 50¢ per book in the U.S. and 75¢ per book in Canada.* I understand that accepting the 2 free books and gifts places me under no obligation to buy anything. I can always return a shipment and cancel at any time. Even if I never buy another book, the two free books and gifts are mine to keep forever.

194/394 MDN FELQ

Name	(PLEASE PRINT)

Address	Apt. #

City	State/Prov.	Zip/Postal Code

Signature (if under 18, a parent or guardian must sign)

Mail to the Reader Service:
IN U.S.A.: P.O. Box 1867, Buffalo, NY 14240-1867
IN CANADA: P.O. Box 609, Fort Erie, Ontario L2A 5X3

Not valid for current subscribers to the Romance Collection
or the Romance/Suspense Collection.

**Want to try two free books from another line?
Call 1-800-873-8635 or visit www.ReaderService.com.**

* Terms and prices subject to change without notice. Prices do not include applicable taxes. Sales tax applicable in N.Y. Canadian residents will be charged applicable taxes. Offer not valid in Quebec. This offer is limited to one order per household. All orders subject to credit approval. Credit or debit balances in a customer's account(s) may be offset by any other outstanding balance owed by or to the customer. Please allow 4 to 6 weeks for delivery. Offer available while quantities last.

Your Privacy—The Reader Service is committed to protecting your privacy. Our Privacy Policy is available online at www.ReaderService.com or upon request from the Reader Service.

We make a portion of our mailing list available to reputable third parties that offer products we believe may interest you. If you prefer that we not exchange your name with third parties, or if you wish to clarify or modify your communication preferences, please visit us at www.ReaderService.com/consumerchoice or write to us at Reader Service Preference Service, P.O. Box 9062, Buffalo, NY 14269. Include your complete name and address.

ROM11

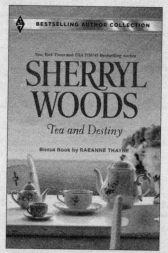